BURIED SECRETS

A HARRY STARKE STORY

BLAIR HOWARD

Printed Cleveland, TN, USA
Print Paperback ISBN: 979-8-9988024-1-6
Blair Howard Books
BlairHoward@BlairHowardBooks.com

PREFACE

Some secrets don't stay buried.

In 2017 when Eleanor Reynolds walked into Harry Starke's office with only months to live, she made one final request: find out what happened to her son who vanished fifteen years ago without a trace.

Reluctantly, Harry takes the cold case, knowing it's probably cold for good reason: lack of evidence. But his investigation uncovers disturbing connections between Michael Reynold's disappearance and four of Chattanooga's most powerful men, men who will stop at nothing to make sure the past stays buried.

In a race against time and ruthless enemies, Harry must uncover the truth before it's silenced forever.

Will he find justice for a dying mother? Or will he become the next victim of a fifteen-year conspiracy?

CHAPTER 1

The Visitor

IT WAS A DARK AND DREARY MONDAY MORNING IN MID-OCTOBER 2019. Rain lashed against the windows of my office on the ground floor of the Flatiron Building in downtown Chattanooga. The weather matched my mood. I'd spent Sunday night at The Sorbonne, Benny Hinkle's seedy excuse for a nightclub, following a cheating husband for a client who refused to believe her old man was playing around until I shoved the evidence under her nose. Now I was nursing a headache from the brain-numbing noise Benny called music while contemplating a mountain of paperwork.

I was dressed for work: black tee, black leather jacket, black jeans, and heavy black leather boots. My S&W MP9 rode in its holster at my hip. Sound corny? I agree, it does, but it's a uniform designed to give people the wrong impression about me, which is exactly how I like it. First impressions can give me a big advantage.

Jacque Hale, my Jamaican PA, appeared in the doorway. She was, as always, impeccably dressed in a charcoal gray pantsuit that contrasted beautifully with a cream-colored silk blouse. At thirty, she looked nineteen, with bushy black hair framing a face that lit up the room when she smiled, but she wasn't smiling now.

"Harry, there's someone here to see you," she said.

I glanced at my watch and frowned. "I don't have any appointments until this afternoon."

"It's a walk-in. An elderly woman. She seems... determined."

I sighed and ran a hand through my hair. "Geez," I muttered. "What does she want?"

"She wouldn't say. Just that it's personal and urgent."

I nodded. "Give me five minutes, then send her in."

After Jacque left, I straightened my desk, which meant closing the open files, shoving them into a drawer and closing my laptop. Walk-ins were rarely worth my time those days, but there was something in Jacque's tone that made me curious.

Five minutes later, there was a soft knock on the door, and Jacque ushered in a small, elderly woman. She was thin, looked frail, but carried herself with dignity. Her silver hair was pulled back into a neat bun, and despite the rain, her navy-blue dress and matching coat were immaculate. I guessed her to be in her seventies, though the lines on her face suggested she'd seen more than her fair share of hardship.

I stood and gestured to the chair across from my desk. "Please, have a seat, Mrs...?"

"Reynolds. Eleanor Reynolds," she said, her voice surprisingly firm. She lowered herself carefully into the chair, placing her handbag on her lap and a weathered cardboard box at her feet.

"What can I do for you, Mrs. Reynolds?"

She looked directly into my eyes, and I saw a steely determination there that belied her fragile appearance.

"Mr. Starke, my son Michael disappeared fifteen years ago. The police investigated, but nothing came of it. The case went cold. They eventually concluded he must have left town voluntarily, but I never believed that. Not for a moment."

I leaned back in my chair, studying her. "Fifteen years is a long time, Mrs. Reynolds. What makes you come looking for answers now?"

She held my gaze. "I'm dying, Mr. Starke. Cancer. The doctors give me three to four months. Before I go, I need to know what happened to my son."

The bluntness of her statement caught me off guard. I've dealt with all sorts of over my years, both as a cop and then a PI —the wealthy, the desperate, the vengeful—but there was something about Eleanor Reynolds that commanded respect.

"I'm sorry to hear that," I said, meaning it. "But I have to ask; what do you expect me to find that the police couldn't?"

She reached down and lifted the cardboard box onto my desk with surprising strength. "The police were busy. There was that serial killer operating in Chattanooga that year, and they had other priorities. Michael's case... it just faded away." She pushed the box toward me. "This is everything I have of Michael's that might help. Including his journal."

I opened the box. Inside were photos, letters, a few personal items, and a leather-bound notebook.

"Michael was an engineer at Chattanooga Manufacturing Industries," Eleanor continued. "He was twenty-eight when he vanished. The week before he disappeared, he was agitated, working late, making cryptic phone calls. He told me he'd discovered something at work, something wrong, but wouldn't elaborate."

I picked up the journal and flipped through it. The last few pages contained what looked like account numbers, dates, and dollar amounts, along with hastily scribbled notes that made little sense out of context.

"What do you think happened to him?" I asked.

Her hands tightened on her handbag. "I think someone wanted to silence him, Mr. Starke. And I think they succeeded."

I closed the journal and looked at her. "Mrs. Reynolds, I need to be straight with you. Cold cases like this—especially after fifteen years—they're difficult to solve. The trail is beyond cold; it's practically frozen. And my services aren't cheap."

She nodded. "I understand. Money isn't an issue. I've sold my house to move into hospice care. What's left is for finding Michael." She pulled an envelope from her handbag and placed it on the desk. "This is a retainer. Ten thousand dollars. Will that do to start?"

I didn't touch the envelope. "Why me?" I asked.

A faint smile touched her lips. "Your reputation, Mr. Starke. I asked around. They say you're the best. They say you don't give up. They say you get results when others can't." The smile faded. "And I don't have time for second best."

Now I've never been one to turn down a challenge, especially when it involves a puzzle that others have failed to solve. And there was something about Eleanor Reynolds that got to me—her quiet dignity, her determination to find closure before time ran out.

I picked up the envelope and nodded. "Alright, Mrs. Reynolds. I'll take your case. I can't promise miracles, but I'll do everything I can to find out what happened to your son."

Relief washed over her face, softening the lines momentarily. "Thank you, Mr. Starke."

I stood and walked around the desk. "I'll need your contact information, and the name of someone I can talk to if you're... unavailable."

"Of course." She opened her bag and handed me a card with her details. "My hospice information is there, and my nephew's number. Thomas will handle my affairs when... well, when the time comes."

I took the card. "I'll keep you updated on any progress. And

Mrs. Reynolds, I rarely do this, but given your situation, I'll prioritize this case."

She rose slowly to her feet. "I appreciate that, Mr. Starke. Time isn't on my side."

As I led her to the door, she stopped and looked up at me. "There's one more thing you should know. Two days ago, I received an anonymous phone call. A man's voice. He said, 'Let sleeping dogs lie, Eleanor.' Then he hung up."

"You didn't mention this to the police?"

She shook her head. "What would be the point? They've written Michael off as a voluntary disappearance. Besides," her eyes hardened, "it tells me I'm right. Someone doesn't want the truth to come out."

I opened the door. "I'll walk you out," I said.

"No need," she replied. "Your assistant already offered to call me a taxi. I may be dying, Mr. Starke, but I'm not helpless. Not yet."

I watched as she walked steadily to Jacque's desk. Despite her age and illness, Eleanor Reynolds had a core of steel, and I respected that.

Jacque caught my eye over the older woman's head and raised an eyebrow in silent question. I nodded, and she gave me a small smile before turning her attention back to Mrs. Reynolds.

I returned to my office and sat behind my desk, pulling the journal from the box. The last entry was dated August 17, 2002. Fifteen years was a hell of a long time. Witnesses would have moved on or died. Evidence would be gone. Memories would have faded. But secrets... secrets had a way of enduring.

I flipped through the journal again, stopping at a page with hurriedly scrawled notes: "CMI accounts don't match. Harmon knows. Meeting tomorrow. Evidence secure."

Tomorrow never came for Michael Reynolds, at least not the tomorrow he was expecting.

I pulled out my phone and dialed an internal number.

"Tim, I need you in my office. Bring TJ too. We've got a new case."

I hung up and stared at the journal. Fifteen years was a long time for secrets to stay buried. But no secret stays buried forever. And then there was the phone call she received: 'Let sleeping dogs lie, Eleanor.' Someone was worried, and I had a feeling that this one was about to resurface in a big way.

Eleanor Reynolds deserved answers. And I was going to find them for her.

CHAPTER 2

Cold Trail

TEN MINUTES AFTER ELEANOR REYNOLDS LEFT MY OFFICE, TIM Clarke and TJ Bron were seated across from me. Tim, my computer wizard, looked like he always did—tall, skinny, with thick glasses perched on the end of his nose, dressed in a wrinkled button-down and jeans that hung off his 150-pound frame, laptop on his knee, phone on the edge of my desk. He still looked like a teenager, but his mind operated in a digital realm few could access. He'd been with me since he was seventeen, when I'd found him at an internet café shortly after he'd dropped out of college, one step ahead of the law for his hacking activities.

Next to him sat TJ Bron, a study in contrasts. TJ was the oldest member of my team, but his military background kept him in better shape than men half his age. Six feet tall with white hair and a deeply tanned, lined face that spoke of hard years, he carried himself with the quiet dignity of a man who had seen too much. A highly decorated Vietnam vet and former Marine—I know, I know. There's no such thing as a former Marine—he'd joined my team after a crooked bank officer had framed him, resulting in jail time that cost him everything—his career, family, and home. Kate Gazzara, a detective friend of mine, had found him homeless three months earlier and brought him to me. His background in accounting made him perfect as my financial investigator and now my lead investigator.

"What's up, boss?" Tim asked, already fidgeting with his phone. The kid couldn't keep still when there was potential data to mine.

I gestured to the box on my desk. "We have a new case. Cold as they come."

"How cold?" TJ asked, his voice carrying the gravelly edge of a lifetime smoker, though he'd quit years ago.

"Fifteen years," I replied. "Missing person, presumed dead. Michael Reynolds, twenty-eight, engineer at Chattanooga Manufacturing Industries. Disappeared August 2002 after allegedly discovering financial irregularities at the company."

Tim whistled. "Fifteen years? That's practically prehistoric in digital terms."

"Which is why I need you both." I pulled the journal from the box and handed it to TJ. "Michael's mother just hired us. She's dying—terminal cancer—and wants answers before she goes."

TJ took the journal carefully. "What did the police find back then?"

"Not much, apparently," I replied. "There was a serial killer operating in Chattanooga that year stretching resources thin—The Riverside Strangler. Remember him? The Reynolds' case went cold. They eventually filed it as a voluntary disappearance."

"But you don't think so," TJ said. It wasn't a question.

"No, especially after she told me about a call she received a couple of days ago. 'Let sleeping dogs lie, Eleanor,' and no, she didn't recognize the voice. And there's this." I gestured to the journal. "The last few entries mention accounting discrepancies at CMI, meetings with someone named Harmon, and securing evidence."

TJ nodded, already flipping through the pages. "I see some account numbers here. Financial codes. I recognize the structure from my banking days."

"Tim, I need you to dig into CMI's history—personnel, financial reports, news stories, anything about the company from fifteen years ago, particularly around August 2002. Look for any executives or employees named Harmon. Also check for recent activity—real estate development, acquisitions, anything that might stir up old business."

Tim nodded, already typing notes on his laptop. "On it. Should be able to access SEC filings and public records. What about internal documents?"

"Do what you can legally." I gave him a pointed look. "At least for now."

He understood the implication. Tim's hacking skills were a tool I used sparingly and only when absolutely necessary.

"TJ, I want you to analyze those journal entries. See if you can make sense of the financial references. Also, get a list of former CMI employees from that period. We need to track down potential witnesses."

"What about this Harmon character?" TJ asked.

"I'll start there. Also, I want to review the original police investigation. Fortunately, I still have friends in the department who can help with that."

Jacque appeared at the door, her face serious. "I've pulled all the public records on Michael Reynolds' disappearance. There's not much. Just a small article in the Times Free Press. A missing person report. No follow-up stories."

"What about his family?" I asked.

"Mother, Eleanor, we just met. The father died when Michael was twelve. There's one younger brother, Thomas, who would have been a teenager when Michael disappeared. He's currently a journalist for the Atlanta Constitution."

I nodded. "Get in touch with the brother. Carefully. Tell him we're investigating his brother's case at his mother's request, but don't mention her condition unless he already knows."

"Already texted him. He's in Sierra Leone on assignment but says he'll call when he gets to a secure connection."

This was why Jacque was worth her weight in gold; always three steps ahead.

"Great. Also, see if you can track down the detective who handled the original case."

"Walter Morris," she said, consulting her tablet. "Retired four years ago. Lives in Red Bank. I have his number."

I smiled. "You're a wonder, Jacque."

She returned the smile briefly before her professional demeanor returned. "I try. Anything else?"

"That's it for now. Let's meet back here at four to compare notes."

After Jacque and Tim left, TJ remained, still examining the journal.

"Something on your mind, TJ?" I asked.

He looked up, his eyes sharp despite his years. "This isn't just about money, Harry."

"What do you mean?"

"These notes..." He tapped the journal. "Reynolds was methodical, organized. An engineer's mind. But these last entries—they're erratic, hurried. He was scared."

I leaned forward. "Scared enough to disappear on his own?"

TJ shook his head. "No. Scared enough to get himself killed." He closed the journal carefully. "I've seen financial fraud cases before. Worked a few at the bank before everything went south for me. The numbers rarely justify murder unless there's something bigger at stake."

"Like what?"

"Power. Position. Reputation." He stood up slowly, tucking the journal under his arm. "I'll dig into these accounts and see what our boy Michael found that was worth dying for."

After TJ left, I sat back in my chair, contemplating the case. Fifteen years was a long time, but TJ was right—some motives never expire.

I picked up the phone and dialed a number I knew by heart.

"Detective Morris? This is Harry Starke. I need to talk to you about an old case of yours. Michael Reynolds."

WALTER MORRIS HAD AGED EXACTLY as you'd expect a retired detective to age—poorly, with a face mapped by stress lines and eyes that had seen too much of human depravity. We sat at a corner table in The Blue Fox, a bar just off Amnicola Highway that catered to off-duty cops. Morris nursed a bourbon, neat, while I stuck to club soda. It was only noon, and I had work to do.

"Michael Reynolds," Morris said, rolling the name around like he was tasting it. "Now there's a name I haven't heard in years. Went missing, what, 2002?"

"August 17, 2002," I confirmed. "You caught the case."

Morris nodded, his gray crew cut catching the dim light. "Yeah, I remember. An engineer, lived alone, good job at CMI. His mother reported him missing after he didn't show for Sunday dinner and wasn't answering his phone."

"What did you find?"

Morris took a slow sip of his bourbon. "Not much. No signs of forced entry at his apartment. His car was gone. We found it at the airport long-term parking. No activity on his credit cards or bank accounts after he disappeared. No airline tickets purchased under his name."

"You think he ran?"

Morris set his glass down. "At the time, it made sense. We were up to our eyeballs in the Riverside Strangler cases. Four women dead, media breathing down our necks. Reynolds was an adult male with no signs of foul play. His disappearance checked all the boxes for voluntary."

"But?" I prompted, hearing the hesitation in his voice.

"But it never sat right." Morris leaned forward. "Not with me. His apartment; it was too neat. Nothing missing except his passport. No clothes packed, no personal items taken. Who leaves town permanently and doesn't pack underwear?"

"You think someone staged it to look like he left?" I asked.

"I didn't say that." Morris glanced around, an old cop's habit. "What I'm saying is, the case got moved to the back burner. By the time we caught the Strangler, Reynolds had been gone three months. The trail was cold. My lieutenant told me to file it, forget it, and move on."

"His mother mentioned he'd been anxious the week before," I said. "She said he'd discovered something funny going on at work."

Morris nodded. "She told me the same thing. I checked with his supervisor at CMI. Guy said Reynolds had been working on some efficiency project, nothing secret or controversial. His colleagues described him as quiet, dedicated, not the type to make waves."

"But somebody made a call to the mother recently," I said. "Warning her to 'let sleeping dogs lie.'"

Morris's eyes narrowed. "That's new. When was this?"

"Two days ago."

He whistled low. "Fifteen years later, huh? Somebody's nervous."

"About what, though? What could a junior engineer have found that's still worth keeping quiet after all this time?"

Morris finished his bourbon in one swallow. "That's your

problem now, Harry. But I'll tell you this; the airport security footage from that week was corrupted. Technical glitch, they said. We never got a clean look at who parked Reynolds' car there."

I sat up straighter. "That wasn't in the report."

"No, it wasn't." Morris fixed me with a level stare. "Because two days after I requested a forensic recovery of that footage, my lieutenant told me the case was officially classified as a voluntary disappearance, and any further resources spent on it would come out of my pension."

"That sounds like pressure from above."

"It sure as hell wasn't standard procedure." Morris stood, reaching for his jacket. "Look, I'm retired now. Got nothing to lose. If you find something, I want to know."

I nodded. "I'll keep you in the loop."

As Morris walked toward the door, he paused. "One more thing, Harry. Reynolds' supervisor at CMI? A man named Victor Harmon. Last I heard, he's some big shot businessman now. Might be worth looking into."

After Morris left, I sat for a while, thinking. A missing engineer. Corrupted security footage. A lieutenant shutting down an investigation. And a name—Victor Harmon—that appeared in Michael's journal.

The cold trail was heating up.

I paid the tab and headed back to my office. I needed to see what Tim and TJ had found. And I needed to locate Victor Harmon.

The case that had gone cold fifteen years ago was about to become very hot indeed.

CHAPTER 3

Digital Breadcrumbs

BY THE TIME I GOT BACK TO THE OFFICE, TIM WAS HUNCHED over his array of screens, his fingers flying across the keyboard with the speed and precision of a concert pianist. His workspace resembled the bridge of a spaceship: four huge flat screens arranged in a grid, displaying windows of code, financial charts, and corporate documents that made about as much sense to me as hieroglyphics.

I leaned against the doorframe, watching him work. Tim was in his element, lost in the digital realm, where he reigned supreme. This was why I'd spent over fifty-five grand on his setup. The three Dell towers hummed quietly in the corner, processing the power that Tim wielded like a virtuoso.

"Find anything interesting?" I asked.

Tim didn't look up, his fingers continuing their dance across the keyboard. "Define 'interesting.' If by 'interesting' you mean suspicious financial patterns at CMI during 2002 and 2002, then yes. If by 'interesting' you mean the meteoric rise of several CMI executives following a company restructuring in late 2002, then definitely yes."

I stepped into the room, my interest piqued. "Show me," I said.

Tim swiveled in his chair and pointed to the upper left screen. "This is CMI's quarterly financial reporting from 1998 to 2002. See these dips here in late 2002?" He traced a downward trend on a graph. "The company reported manufacturing losses, equipment failures, and inventory shrinkage."

"What does that mean in English?"

Tim adjusted his glasses. "It means they were writing off a lot of assets as lost or damaged. But here's the thing—" He switched to another screen showing production reports. "Their output didn't decrease during this period. If anything, they were more productive."

"So they were writing off assets that weren't actually lost."

"Exactly. It's a classic embezzlement setup. You create phantom losses on paper while maintaining or increasing actual production." Tim pulled up another window. "And then, miraculously, in the fourth quarter of 2002—right after Michael Reynolds disappeared—the company's fortunes reversed. Profits increased by twenty-eight percent."

"That's quite a turnaround."

"It gets better." Tim switched to another screen showing a series of news articles and corporate profiles. "Following this financial recovery, several key executives moved on to bigger and better things."

He clicked through a series of headshots.

"Victor Harmon, CFO of CMI at the time of Reynolds' disappearance, left the company in early 2003 to start his own investment firm. Harmon Capital is now one of the largest private equity firms in Tennessee."

Another click. "Diane Lawson, head of accounting, now runs her own successful financial consulting business in Nashville."

Click. "Raymond Powell, head of security, owns Powell

Protection Services, a high-end security firm with contracts for half the corporate buildings in Chattanooga."

Click. "And the crown jewel—James Lucan, former legal counsel for CMI, launched his political career in early 2002 with a surprisingly well-funded campaign for state senate. He's now in his third term, and rumors say he's eyeing the governor's mansion."

"All this happened after Reynolds disappeared?"

"Within eighteen months. It's like they all got a sudden infusion of cash and confidence." Tim leaned back in his chair. "Now, I can't prove they were involved in embezzlement without access to internal records from that time. But the pattern is suspicious as hell."

I studied the faces on the screen—Harmon, with his square jaw and silver-streaked dark hair; Lawson, blonde and polished to a corporate shine; Powell, built like a bulldog with close-cropped hair; and Lucan, with the practiced smile of a politician.

"What about the current CEO? Martin Greene?"

Tim clicked to another profile. "Greene was a rising executive when Reynolds disappeared. He became CEO in 2003 after the previous chief retired. Under his leadership, CMI has doubled in size and expanded into three new states."

"So everyone connected to CMI during that time has prospered," I said.

"Everyone in the executive suite," Tim corrected. "I've been tracking down former employees from the factory floor. Several mentioned a round of layoffs in early 2002—cost-cutting measures, they were told. Interesting timing, considering the financial 'recovery' that followed."

I nodded, processing the information. "What about Reynolds himself? Anything unusual about his personal finances?"

"Nothing obvious. Steady income, modest spending, small

retirement account. No sudden withdrawals or deposits." Tim pushed his glasses up his nose. "But I found something interesting about his work computer."

"Which was?"

"It was reported stolen from his office the day after he was reported missing. Company filed a police report, claiming someone broke into his office over the weekend."

"Convenient."

"Very. Especially since the company-wide security system allegedly malfunctioned that same weekend, resulting in no usable surveillance footage."

I smiled grimly. "Just like the airport footage that was mysteriously corrupted."

Tim raised an eyebrow. "You're thinking what I'm thinking?"

"That someone was very thorough about covering their tracks."

"The thoroughness doesn't stop there." Tim pulled up another window showing property records. "CMI owned a secondary manufacturing facility on the outskirts of town—an older plant they supposedly shut down in 1999 due to 'inefficiency.' The property has changed hands three times since then."

"And?"

"And it's currently owned by the T-River Development Group, which just filed permits to demolish the existing structure and build a commercial complex." Tim swiveled to face me directly. "Want to guess who's a major investor in T-River Development?"

"Victor Harmon?"

"Bingo. And the demolition is scheduled to begin next week."

I straightened up. "That's a hell of a coincidence. A cold case gets stirred up just as they're about to bulldoze a potentially relevant location."

Tim shrugged. "Maybe not such a coincidence. The plans have been public for months. Could be what prompted someone to warn Eleanor Reynolds to back off."

I pulled out my phone and checked the time. "I need to see that property before the bulldozers move in. Anything else I should know?"

"Just one more thing." Tim pulled up a final screen showing a series of offshore bank accounts. "I've been tracing the money trail from CMI during those suspicious quarters. It's complex—shell companies, multiple transfers—but there's a pattern. The funds eventually converged in a Cayman Islands account that was closed in 2003."

"Can you tell who controlled the account?"

Tim grinned, the expression making him look even younger. "Not officially. But I found a connection to an LLC that listed Raymond Powell as a director. He might have been the point man for moving the money."

I clapped Tim on the shoulder. "Good work, Tim. Keep digging. I want to know everything there is to know about these people—Harmon, Lawson, Powell, Lucan, and Greene. Personal histories, current addresses, financial holdings, the works."

"Even if I have to go a bit... gray area?" Tim asked, his eyes gleaming with the challenge.

I sighed and nodded. "Just... be careful. And plausible deniability, remember?"

"Always."

I left Tim to his digital excavation and headed back to my office. Along the way, I passed TJ, who was bent over a desk in the conference room, surrounded by printouts and a legal pad filled with his neat handwriting.

"Make any headway with those journal entries?" I asked.

TJ looked up, his weathered face creased in concentration. "Some. Reynolds was tracking specific transactions—materials purchased but never delivered, equipment written off as damaged but still in use. The boy had a good eye for detail."

"Good enough to get himself killed?"

"Good enough to have seen exactly what someone didn't want seen." TJ held up a page from his legal pad. "I've compiled a list of transactions he flagged. Total comes to just over eight million dollars over an eighteen-month period."

I whistled. "Eight million is a pretty good motive."

"It's also just the tip of the iceberg. These are only the discrepancies Reynolds documented. The actual scheme was likely much larger."

"Any names mentioned with the transactions?"

"Most entries just have initials. 'VH approved delivery write-off.' 'DL adjusted inventory records.' Pretty clear who he was tracking."

"Victor Harmon and Diane Lawson."

TJ nodded. "There are also frequent mentions of 'RP' ensuring security protocols and 'JC' handling legal documentation."

"Raymond Powell and James Lucan. The gang's all here." I frowned. "What about Martin Greene?"

TJ flipped through his notes. "Only one reference. 'MG questioned VH about Q3 numbers. VH assured him everything in order.' If Greene was involved, Reynolds didn't have evidence of it."

"Or Greene was asking legitimate questions and got fed a line."

"Possible." TJ gathered his papers into a neat stack. "There's one more thing. The last entry, dated August 16, 2002—the day before Reynolds disappeared. It says: 'Meeting VH tomorrow. Bringing evidence. This ends now.'"

A chill ran down my spine. "He confronted Harmon."

"Looks that way." TJ's eyes, sharp despite his years, met mine. "And that was the last anyone heard from him."

"Not quite," I said. "According to a retired detective I just spoke with, Reynolds' car was found in the airport long-term parking lot. But the security footage from that day was corrupted."

TJ snorted. "Convenient."

"That's what I said. And Tim just told me the security system at CMI mysteriously malfunctioned the weekend Reynolds disappeared, and his work computer was reported stolen."

"Sounds like a professional cleanup job." TJ's voice carried the gravity of a man who had seen his share of coverups. "Military precision."

"Speaking of cleanup, the old CMI factory where Reynolds worked is scheduled for demolition next week. I want to check it out before the bulldozers move in."

TJ stood, straightening his back with a slight wince. "I'll come with you."

"No need. I want you to focus on tracking down former CMI employees who might have worked with Reynolds. See if anyone remembers him mentioning concerns or acting strangely before he disappeared."

He nodded. "Will do."

As I turned to leave, TJ's voice stopped me. "Harry, whoever these people are, they've had fifteen years to cover their tracks and build their defenses. They're wealthy, connected, and they've already killed once. Be careful."

"Always am," I replied with more confidence than I felt.

Back in my office, I found Jacque waiting with a manila folder.

"I pulled everything I could find on Victor Harmon," she said, handing me the folder. "Current address, business holdings, social schedule. He's speaking at a Chamber of Commerce dinner tomorrow night."

I flipped through the file. Harmon lived in a mansion on Lookout Mountain, maintained offices downtown, and moved in Chattanooga's highest social circles. A long way from his days as a CFO at a manufacturing company.

"Good work. See if you can get me an invitation to that dinner."

Jacque raised an eyebrow. "You hate those events."

"I'll make an exception," I replied dryly.

"I'll see what I can do." She paused at the door. "Oh, and Thomas Reynolds called back. He's cutting his assignment short and flying back to the States. Says he'll be in Chattanooga by Friday."

"Did he say why the sudden interest?"

"Just that he's been looking into his brother's disappearance for years. Something about new information coming to light."

"Did he mention what information?"

She shook her head. "He was being careful. Satellite phone from West Africa isn't exactly secure."

After Jacque left, I sat at my desk, processing everything we'd uncovered. Financial irregularities at CMI. A group of executives who all prospered after Reynolds disappeared. A confrontation the day before he vanished. An abandoned factory scheduled for demolition.

The pieces were starting to form a picture, and it wasn't pretty.

I pulled out my phone and dialed a number.

"Chattanooga PD, Detective Gazzara."

"Kate, it's Harry. I need a favor."

"Why am I not surprised?" Despite her words, I could hear the smile in her voice.

"I need to know if anyone's been asking about a cold case—Michael Reynolds. He disappeared August 2002."

There was a pause, then the sound of a keyboard clicking. "Let me check... Nothing recent in our system. Why?"

"His mother hired me to look into it. Said she received a threatening call warning her to back off."

"Back off from what? The case has been inactive for years."

"That's what I'm trying to figure out." I hesitated, then added, "The old CMI factory where he worked is scheduled for demolition next week."

Kate's voice sharpened. "You think there's evidence there?"

"I think it's worth checking out before it's reduced to rubble."

"Harry..." Her tone carried a warning. "Don't go breaking and entering."

"Would I do that?"

"In a heartbeat." She sighed. "Look, if you find something concrete, bring it to me. I can get a warrant."

"Will do."

"And Harry?"

"Yeah?"

"Be careful. Cold cases sometimes stay cold for a reason."

I hung up and stared out my office window at the Chattanooga skyline. Kate was right—cold cases often stayed cold because powerful people wanted them that way.

But Eleanor Reynolds deserved answers. And I had a feeling those answers were buried at an abandoned factory scheduled for demolition in less than a week.

Time was running out—for the factory, for Eleanor, and possibly for anyone who started digging too deep into the disappearance of Michael Reynolds.

CHAPTER 4

The Ex-Girlfriend

THE NEXT MORNING, I WAS UP EARLY. AFTER A FIVE-MILE RUN along the Tennessee Riverwalk and a quick shower, I dressed more carefully than usual. Instead of my standard black outfit, I put on dark gray slacks, a pale blue shirt with a royal blue tie, and a navy blue blazer—what I called my "IBM look." When you're about to interview a financial professional, it helps to appear like you belong in their world.

TJ met me in the office parking lot at 8:30, looking surprisingly sharp in a charcoal suit that had seen better days but was immaculately pressed. His white hair was neatly combed, and he'd even polished his shoes.

"Nice suit," I commented as he climbed into the passenger seat of my Maxima.

He grunted. "Had it since 2005. Still fits." He tugged at the collar. "Mostly."

I pulled out onto Georgia Avenue. "You've been briefed on Diane Lawson?"

"Former head of accounting at CMI. Now runs Lawson

Financial Solutions in Nashville." TJ pulled a small notebook from his inside pocket. "Forty-six years old, divorced twice, no children. Graduated University of Tennessee with an MBA in finance. Started at CMI in 1995, rose quickly to head of accounting by 1999."

"And she was dating Michael Reynolds."

TJ nodded. "According to his mother the relationship lasted about six months and ended approximately two months before he disappeared." He flipped a page in his notebook. "Tim found something interesting about Ms. Lawson's finances. In November 2002—three months after Reynolds disappeared— she purchased a condo in downtown Nashville for cash. Eight hundred thousand dollars."

I raised an eyebrow. "That's a nice bonus."

"Especially for someone making an estimated one hundred and ten thousand a year at CMI."

"What's her income now?"

"Tax returns show her business clearing north of two million annually." TJ looked over at me. "She's done very well for herself."

"So let's find out how," I muttered.

———

LAWSON FINANCIAL SOLUTIONS occupied a sleek office suite in one of Nashville's newer office towers. The ninety-minute drive from Chattanooga had given me time to consider different approaches. In the end, I decided that a direct confrontation would yield the most telling reactions.

The reception area screamed success—glass and chrome furnishings, abstract art on the walls, a stunning view of downtown Nashville. A poised young woman behind the reception desk greeted us with a practiced smile.

"Welcome to Lawson Financial Solutions. Do you have an appointment?"

I flashed my most disarming smile. "Harry Starke and TJ Bron to see Ms. Lawson. We don't have an appointment, but she'll want to speak with us."

The receptionist's smile didn't falter, but her eyes cooled. "Ms. Lawson's schedule is fully booked today. I'd be happy to make an appointment for next week."

I held her gaze. "Please tell her we're here about Michael Reynolds."

A flicker of uncertainty crossed her face. "One moment." She picked up her phone and murmured something too low for us to hear.

TJ leaned close to me. "She recognized the name," he whispered.

I nodded slightly. The receptionist was having an intense conversation, her professional demeanor slipping as she cast nervous glances our way.

Finally, she hung up and forced a smile back onto her face. "Ms. Lawson has a few minutes between appointments. Please follow me."

She led us down a hallway lined with awards and financial certificates to a corner office with floor-to-ceiling windows. Diane Lawson stood beside a glass desk, her body language telegraphing tension despite her polished appearance.

She was an attractive woman with shoulder-length blonde hair, sharp features, and a figure maintained by expensive gym memberships. Her navy-blue suit probably cost more than most people's monthly mortgage payments. A large diamond glittered on her right hand, and a designer watch adorned her left wrist.

"Gentlemen," she said coolly. "I understand you wished to speak with me about a former colleague."

I studied her face closely. No shock, no confusion—she knew exactly who Michael Reynolds was.

"Thank you for making time, Ms. Lawson. I'm Harry Starke, a private investigator from Chattanooga. This is my associate, TJ Bron."

She didn't offer to shake hands or invite us to sit. "What is this concerning, precisely?" she asked tersely.

"I've been hired by Eleanor Reynolds to investigate her son's disappearance fifteen years ago."

Lawson's expression didn't change, but her right hand moved to touch her necklace—a nervous gesture. "That's a very long time ago, Mr. Starke. I'm not sure how I can help."

"You were dating Michael in the months before he disappeared."

She sighed and gestured to the chairs in front of her desk. "Please, sit down. This is ancient history, but I'll tell you what I told the police back then."

We took our seats. She settled behind her desk, visibly regaining her composure.

"Michael and I dated briefly. It wasn't serious, at least not to me. We ended things amicably about two months before he disappeared." She folded her hands on the desk. "I was as shocked as anyone when he went missing."

"According to his mother, he was troubled in the weeks before his disappearance," I said. "Something about financial irregularities at CMI."

Her expression hardened slightly. "Michael had... anxieties about the company's accounting practices. He didn't understand corporate finance—he was an engineer, not an accountant. I tried to explain standard business practices to him, but he became fixated on certain transactions."

"What kind of transactions?" TJ asked, his voice calm but probing.

Lawson's eyes flickered to his. "Write-offs, primarily.

Equipment depreciation, inventory adjustments—standard accounting procedures, but Michael didn't understand them. He started seeing conspiracies where there were only normal business operations."

"Did he confront anyone about these... misunderstandings?" I asked.

She hesitated, almost imperceptibly. "He mentioned taking his concerns to Victor Harmon, our CFO at the time."

"And how did that go?"

"I wouldn't know. We had already broken up by then." She glanced at her watch. "I'm sorry, but I really do have another appointment in ten minutes."

I leaned forward slightly. "Just a few more questions, Ms. Lawson. How well did you know Victor Harmon back then?"

Her expression remained neutral, but her eyes hardened. "He was the CFO. I reported to him."

"And Raymond Powell? James Lucan?"

"Security and legal counsel, respectively. We worked for the same company, Mr. Starke. Naturally, I knew them."

"All four of you left CMI within two years of Michael's disappearance. Quite a coincidence."

Lawson's professional demeanor cracked slightly. "Is there a question in there somewhere?"

"Where were you on August 17, 2002—the day Michael disappeared?"

Her posture stiffened. "I was at work. All day. Several colleagues can confirm that."

"And that evening?"

"I don't recall. It was fifteen years ago."

TJ spoke up, his weathered face impassive. "Ms. Lawson, in November 2002, you purchased a condo in downtown Nashville for eight hundred thousand dollars. Cash. That's a substantial amount for someone on a CMI executive's salary."

The color drained from her face. "My financial affairs are none of your business. I had investments, savings—"

"Did those investments include the eight million dollars that disappeared from CMI over an eighteen-month period?" I asked quietly.

Lawson stood abruptly. "This interview is over. I don't know what you're implying, but I won't sit here and be accused of... whatever it is you're suggesting."

I remained seated, keeping my voice conversational. "No one's accusing you of anything, Ms. Lawson. We're just trying to understand what happened to Michael Reynolds."

"I do not know what happened to him. Now, if you'll excuse me, I have clients waiting." She reached for her desk phone. "Melissa, please show these gentlemen out."

I stood, handing her my card. "If you remember anything else about that time period, please call me."

She didn't take the card, so I left it on her desk. "One last question—have you stayed in touch with Victor Harmon or any of your other colleagues from CMI?"

"No," she said too quickly. "Our paths rarely cross."

The receptionist appeared at the door, her expression uncertain.

"Thank you for your time, Ms. Lawson," I said, heading for the door. "We'll be in touch."

As TJ and I followed the receptionist back to the lobby, I could feel Lawson's eyes boring into my back.

Once we were in the elevator, TJ let out a low whistle. "She's lying. About pretty much everything."

"Yes, she is." I pressed the button for the parking garage. "Did you notice how she didn't ask how Michael's mother was doing? Not even a perfunctory 'How is Mrs. Reynolds?' Most people would at least pretend to care."

"She also didn't seem surprised that we were investigating a fifteen-year-old disappearance. Almost like she was expecting it."

The elevator doors opened, and we stepped into the parking garage.

"What do you think set her off?" TJ asked as we walked to the car. "The money question?"

"That, and mentioning the names of her old colleagues." I unlocked the Maxima with my remote. "She claimed she doesn't stay in touch with them, but I'd bet good money they're still coordinating."

As pulled out of the parking garage, I glanced in the rearview mirror and noticed a black sedan exiting behind us. "We may have company. Silver Audi, two cars back."

TJ didn't turn around. "Want to lose them?" he asked.

"Not yet. Let's see where this goes."

I drove normally through downtown Nashville, making the occasional random turn. The Audi maintained a consistent distance.

"Definitely following us," TJ confirmed, watching the side mirror. "Professional job, too. Keeping well back, switching lanes occasionally to avoid making it obvious."

"Law enforcement?" I asked.

TJ shook his head. "Private. Police would have two vehicles to avoid losing us."

"Let's see how committed they are," I said.

I took a sudden right turn into a shopping center, then cut quickly through the parking lot and exited from another entrance. The Audi followed smoothly, maintaining distance.

"Dedicated," TJ commented.

"Let's give them something to report back," I said as I pulled into a coffee shop parking lot. "I could use a caffeine boost, anyway."

Inside the coffee shop, we positioned ourselves at a window table with a clear view of the parking lot. The Audi had parked several spaces away, and a man in a dark suit remained behind the wheel.

"Professional driver," TJ noted. "Military bearing. Probably ex-law enforcement or security."

I nodded, sipping my coffee. "Lawson's calling in the troops. Which means we've struck a nerve."

TJ frowned. "If they're mobilizing this quickly, we need to move fast. The factory demolition is scheduled for next week."

"I'm going to check it out tonight."

"Want backup?"

I considered it. TJ was fit for his age, but if there was trouble... "No. I'll handle it. I need you to dig deeper into Lawson. Her statement about not having contact with her former colleagues—we need to verify that."

TJ nodded. "I'll put Tim on it. He can check phone records, emails, social media."

We finished our coffees and returned to the car. The Audi remained in place, its driver watching us.

"Let's head back to Chattanooga," I said. "We've rattled Lawson's cage. Let's see what crawls out."

As we pulled onto the interstate, I monitored the rearview mirror. The Audi followed at a discreet distance.

"Our shadow's still with us," TJ said.

"Good. I want them to report back exactly what we did. A straightforward interview followed by a direct return to Chattanooga. Nothing suspicious."

"What are you planning?" he asked.

I smiled grimly. "They'll expect us to pursue this systematically; interviewing suspects one by one, gathering information gradually. What they won't expect is for me to jump straight to the most likely crime scene."

"The factory."

"Tonight."

TJ looked concerned. "Alone?"

"Better that way. Less chance of detection."

"These people have killed before, Harry."

"All the more reason to get to that factory before the evidence is destroyed." I pressed harder on the accelerator, the Maxima's modified engine responding instantly. "If Michael Reynolds is buried on that property, I'm going to find him before those bulldozers arrive."

The Audi fell back slightly but maintained pursuit. I let them follow. By tonight, I'd be somewhere else entirely.

As we crossed the state line back into Tennessee, my phone rang. It was Tim.

"Boss, you need to get back here," he said, his voice tense. "I've been monitoring Lawson's communications since you left her office."

"And?" I asked.

"She made three calls immediately after your meeting. One to Victor Harmon, one to Raymond Powell, and one to a burner phone I can't trace. The calls lasted less than a minute each."

"She's warning them," I said.

"That's not all," Tim continued. "I hacked into CMI's current servers looking for archival material. Someone else is in the system, deleting old files from 2002. They're doing a systematic purge of everything related to that time period."

I exchanged a glance with TJ. "How fast can you download what's left?"

"I'm already on it, but they've got a head start. Whatever was in those files, they're determined to erase it completely."

"Keep at it. We're about an hour out."

I hung up and pressed harder on the gas. The game had changed. Our quiet investigation into a cold case had just become a race against time.

Behind us, the Audi sped up too, maintaining its distance. They weren't even pretending anymore.

"They're scared," TJ said quietly.

"They should be," I replied, thinking of Eleanor Reynolds and her dying wish for answers. "Because I'm not stopping until I find out what happened to Michael Reynolds."

And if that meant breaking into an abandoned factory in the dead of night, so be it. Some secrets are worth the risk to uncover.

CHAPTER 5

Power Players

BY THE TIME I RETURNED TO THE OFFICE, JACQUE HAD WORKED her magic.

"You're all set for the Chamber of Commerce dinner tonight," she announced, handing me an embossed invitation. "Seven o'clock at the Chattanooga Convention Center. Black tie optional, but in your case, mandatory."

I grimaced. So the factory visit was off, at least for tonight. "You know how I feel about monkey suits."

"Which is why I had your tuxedo picked up from the cleaners." Her expression brooked no argument. "You can't go to the Chamber's annual awards dinner dressed like you're about to kick in someone's door."

"Even if that's exactly what I want to do to Victor Harmon?" I asked.

She ignored that. "Your father called. He'll meet you there at six-thirty for drinks beforehand."

I raised an eyebrow. "You called my father?"

"You need a credible reason to be at that dinner. You're not exactly known for your civic involvement." She handed me a folder. "Your cover story is this: You're considering expanding your business, possibly opening a branch in Nashville, and wanted to network with potential clients."

This was why Jacque was irreplaceable. She didn't just execute tasks; she anticipated problems and solved them before they arose.

"What did Tim find after our Lawson interview?" I asked.

"He's in his digital cave, muttering about encrypted files and backup servers. He said he'll brief you before you leave."

I checked my watch. Four-thirty. Not much time to prepare.

"Any word from our tail after we left Nashville?" I asked.

"Tim tracked the Audi back to Powell Protection Services," she replied. "It's registered to the company fleet."

"So Raymond Powell is monitoring us directly."

"It gets better," Jacque said, leading me toward Tim's office. "State Senator Lucan's office called the police commissioner this morning. Wanted to know if there was any 'unusual activity' around the old Reynolds' disappearance."

"And the commissioner called you?" I asked.

She flashed a smile. "His assistant did. We have history."

Again, irreplaceable.

Tim was hunched over his keyboards when we entered, his glasses reflecting the glow of his monitors. He glanced up briefly.

"They're good," he said without preamble. "Professional-grade deletion, including server backups. But they made one mistake."

"And that was?" I asked.

"They didn't account for me." He grinned as he gestured to one of his screens, which displayed a complex directory of files. "I recovered some fragments from an old CMI accounting server that hadn't been properly scrubbed. Mostly metadata, file names, access logs."

"Anything useful?" I asked.

"Very. There was a hidden directory labeled 'Special Projects' that only three user accounts had access to: Harmon's, Lawson's, and someone with the username 'JLUC'—"

"James Lucan," I supplied.

"Right. The directory contained files with names like 'Offshore Holdings,' 'Cayman Transfer Protocol,' and 'Distribution Schedule.' Classic embezzlement infrastructure." He pushed his glasses up his nose. "But the most interesting file was called 'Reynolds Problem.'"

I felt a chill. "Created when?"

"August 15, 2002. Two days before Michael disappeared."

"Can you recover the contents?" I asked.

Tim shook his head. "They did a secure wipe. Seven passes. Whatever was in that file, they really didn't want anyone finding it."

"What about the factory demolition?" I asked.

"Still scheduled for Monday morning." Tim swiveled to another screen. "I pulled the building plans from the county archives. The original factory was built in 1975, renovated in 1992, and partially remodeled in 1999—just before CMI claimed it was 'inefficient' and shut it down."

"What kind of remodeling?" I asked.

"That's the interesting part," Tim replied. "They reinforced the concrete floor in one section of the building—the northwest corner. According to the permits, it was to support new heavy machinery, but no machinery was ever installed. The factory closed three months after the renovation."

"They reinforced the floor, then closed the factory." I considered the implications. "If you wanted to bury something under concrete, you'd want it to be strong enough not to crack or settle visibly."

"Exactly what I was thinking." Tim pulled up satellite images of the property. "The building's been vacant for fifteen years, but there are signs of activity. Security patrols twice daily by Powell Protection Services, and a new perimeter fence installed last month when the demolition was announced."

"They're guarding an empty building?"

"Apparently, its contents are still valuable to someone."

I checked my watch again. "I need to get ready for this dinner. Keep digging. Find me floor plans of that factory with the reinforced section clearly marked."

"Already printing," Tim said, gesturing to a printout emerging from his laser printer. "And there's one more thing you should know about tonight's dinner."

"What's that?" I asked.

"State Senator Lucan is receiving the Chamber's Public Service Award. He'll be seated at the same head table as Harmon."

"Two birds, one stone," I murmured. "Let's see how they react when I show up on their radar."

THE CHATTANOOGA CONVENTION Center was ablaze with lights, the circular drive clogged with luxury vehicles disgorging the city's elite. I pulled my Maxima up to the valet station, drawing skeptical looks until the attendant saw me in my tuxedo. Amazing how differently people treat you based on what you're wearing.

I'd always hated formal wear, but I had to admit that I cleaned up well when required. The tuxedo was bespoke, tailored during a phase when I was dating a socialite who insisted I needed "proper evening attire." The relationship had lasted six months; the tuxedo had endured.

My father was waiting in the lobby, a tumbler of scotch already in hand. August Starke cut an imposing figure in his tuxedo, tall and distinguished with silver hair and the confident bearing of a man accustomed to commanding attention.

His firm—Starke Law—was one of the most successful personal injury practices in three states, thanks to his aggressive advertising and even more aggressive litigation.

"Harry," he greeted me, extending his hand. "You're looking almost respectable."

"Don't get used to it," I replied, shaking his hand firmly.

He glanced around the crowded lobby. "Jacque mentioned you have an interest in tonight's festivities. Something about Victor Harmon?"

"Just doing some background research on a case."

My father raised an eyebrow. "The Reynolds disappearance? It's a bit old to be stirring up now, isn't it?"

I shouldn't have been surprised he knew. My father made it his business to know everything happening in Chattanooga's legal circles.

"His mother is dying," I replied. "She wants closure."

"Understandable." He sipped his scotch. "You should know that Harmon is a major donor to several political campaigns, including James Lucan's. He has friends in high places."

"So I've gathered."

My father studied me over the rim of his glass. "Just be careful, son. Men like Harmon didn't get where they are by being careless."

"Noted," I said.

The doors to the main ballroom opened, and the crowd began to move inside. My father handed me his empty glass.

"I'm at table three with the mayor. You're at twenty-seven, near the back. It was the best I could do on short notice. Good hunting."

He moved away, immediately intercepted by a judge and his wife. I watched him slip effortlessly into networking mode, all smiles and firm handshakes. In another life, August Starke might have been a politician himself. As it was, he was an extremely sharp tort lawyer with a six golf handicap.

Inside the ballroom, crystal chandeliers cast a warm glow over dozens of round tables draped in white linen. A stage dominated the front of the room, flanked by large screens displaying the Chamber of Commerce logo. The head table was on a slightly raised platform, already occupied by the evening's honorees and speakers.

I spotted Victor Harmon immediately. In person, he looked even more imposing than in his photographs: tall and broad-shouldered, with silver-streaked dark hair and a face that radiated authority. He was engaged in conversation with a woman in a blue evening gown, his expression animated.

Beside him sat State Senator James Lucan, leaner and sharper-featured, with the practiced smile of a politician. His hair was a carefully maintained shade of brown that was probably assisted by his stylist, and his eyes constantly scanned the room, noting who was present and who was speaking to whom.

I made my way to my assigned table, introducing myself to the assorted business owners and corporate representatives who were seated there. None of them knew me, which was perfect. I needed to be forgettable to most of the room.

Dinner was served—some kind of chicken dish that I barely tasted—while various Chamber officials made speeches about economic growth and community development. I kept my attention on the head table, particularly on Harmon and Lucan.

During the main course, I noticed Harmon check his phone, frown slightly, and lean over to whisper something to Lucan. The senator's expression didn't change, but he casually scanned the room, his eyes passing over me without recognition.

The moment the dessert plates were cleared, I excused myself from the table and made my way toward the bar set up in the corner of the ballroom. It gave me a clear view of the head table while allowing me to appear occupied.

"Scotch, neat," I told the bartender.

"Make that two," came a voice from beside me. "Put them both on my tab."

I turned to find Victor Harmon standing there, an artificial smile fixed on his face. Up close, I could see the hardness in his eyes that his publicity photos concealed.

"Victor Harmon," he said, extending his hand. "I don't believe we've met."

"Harry Starke." I shook his hand, noting the firmness of his grip—calculated to assert dominance.

"Starke?" His eyes narrowed slightly. "Any relation to August Starke?"

"He's my father."

Harmon's smile widened, but didn't reach his eyes. "I see. Following in the family legal tradition?"

"Not exactly. I run a private investigation agency."

I observed his reaction. The smile remained fixed, but a muscle twitched in his jaw.

"Fascinating field. What brings you to our little Chamber gathering? Looking for clients?"

The bartender set our drinks down. Harmon lifted his glass in a subtle toast.

"Always," I replied, raising my glass. "Though I already have a full caseload. Mostly routine work—background checks, insurance fraud, the occasional missing person."

His eyes locked on mine. "Missing persons can be challenging. Often they don't want to be found."

"True. But sometimes they didn't leave voluntarily."

Harmon took a slow sip of his scotch. "You seem to have a specific case in mind."

"I do, actually. A fifteen-year-old disappearance. A young engineer from CMI—Michael Reynolds. I believe you knew him."

To his credit, Harmon didn't flinch. "The name sounds

vaguely familiar. I dealt with hundreds of employees in my time at CMI."

"He reported directly to you. And disappeared two days after scheduling a meeting with you about financial irregularities he'd discovered."

Harmon's expression hardened. "I think you're mistaken, Mr. Starke. And I find your insinuation offensive."

"No insinuation intended," I said, easily. "Just establishing the facts."

He set his glass down, untouched. "I'm not sure what game you're playing, Starke, but if you're suggesting I had something to do with an employee's disappearance fifteen years ago, you're on very dangerous ground."

"Legally speaking? Or personally?"

His eyes turned to ice. "Both. I'd advise you to drop whatever misguided investigation you're conducting. For your own good."

"Threatening a licensed investigator isn't wise, Mr. Harmon."

"Neither is harassing a respected businessman based on ancient history and conspiracy theories." He leaned closer. "Whatever you think you know, you can't prove. And you can't afford the legal battle that would follow any public accusations."

"I'm not making accusations," I replied. "I'm just asking questions. "

"Ask them somewhere else." Harmon straightened his tie. "I have a speech to give."

As he turned to leave, I said quietly, "One last question—when's the last time you spoke with Diane Lawson?"

He froze for just a heartbeat, then continued walking away without responding.

I sipped my scotch, watching him return to the head table.

He leaned over to whisper something to Senator Lucan, who glanced in my direction with a frown.

My phone vibrated in my pocket. A text from TJ: "Powell Protection car outside convention center. Black Suburban, two men inside."

So they were monitoring me here too," I said, thoughtfully. "Interesting.

The Chamber president took the podium, introducing Senator Lucan as the recipient of the Public Service Award. Polite applause filled the room as Lucan approached the microphone, his politician's smile firmly in place.

"Thank you all for this tremendous honor," he began. "Public service has always been my highest calling..."

I tuned out the platitudes, focusing instead on Harmon, who was watching me from the head table. Our brief conversation had rattled him, despite his cool demeanor. The mention of Diane Lawson had struck a nerve.

After Lucan's acceptance speech, Victor Harmon was introduced as the keynote speaker. He approached the podium with confidence, launching into a well-rehearsed address about economic development and community investment.

Midway through his speech, I felt a presence beside me. A man in a dark suit with the unmistakable bulge of a shoulder holster beneath his jacket.

"Mr. Starke," he said quietly. "I'm with event security. There's a situation requiring your attention outside."

I knew there was no "situation," but I was curious to see where this would lead. I followed him out of the ballroom and into a quiet corridor.

"What's the problem?" I asked, already knowing.

The man dropped the pretense. "Mr. Powell would like a word with you."

Raymond Powell. So he was here too.

"Lead the way."

He directed me to a small conference room off the main corridor. Inside, Raymond Powell waited, a stocky man with close-cropped gray hair and the alert posture of someone with a military or law enforcement background. He wore an expensive suit that couldn't quite disguise his bulldog physique.

"Mr. Starke," Powell said as the door closed behind me. "I understand you've been asking questions about old CMI business."

"Word travels fast," I replied.

"It's my job to know things." Powell remained standing, hands clasped in front of him. "Especially when those things concern my clients."

"And which client are you representing at the moment? Harmon? Lucan? Or are you here on behalf of the whole conspiracy?"

Powell's expression didn't change. "Conspiracy is a serious allegation, Mr. Starke. The kind that requires evidence."

"I'm working on that," I said with a smile.

"Are you? From what I hear, you're working on a wild goose chase for a dying old woman." He took a step closer. "Let me give you some friendly advice. The Reynolds case is closed. Has been for fifteen years. Pursuing it now can only cause pain."

"For whom?" I asked.

"For everyone involved." Powell's voice remained even. "Including you."

I met his gaze. "Is that a threat?"

"A reality check. You're poking your nose into matters that were resolved long ago. No good can come of it."

"A young man disappeared," I said. "His mother deserves to know what happened to him."

Powell sighed, as if dealing with an unreasonable child. "Sometimes the truth doesn't provide the closure people think it will. Sometimes it's better to let sleeping dogs lie."

His choice of words sent a chill through me. "That's exactly what the anonymous caller told Eleanor Reynolds two days ago."

Powell's eyes narrowed slightly—the first genuine reaction I'd seen from him. "Is that so?"

"Word for word. Strange coincidence."

"I wouldn't know anything about that." He adjusted his cuffs. "My interest is simply in preventing unnecessary complications for my clients."

"And in keeping secrets buried? Perhaps literally?"

Powell's jaw tightened. "You're on dangerous ground, Starke."

"So people keep telling me." I moved toward the door. "If there's nothing else, I should get back to the dinner."

"One more thing." Powell's voice stopped me. "I understand you've been looking into the old CMI factory property."

I turned back. "Just curious about the demolition schedule."

"That property is secured and patrolled around the clock," he said. "Trespassing would be unwise and probably unhealthy."

There it was—the direct threat I'd been waiting for.

"Noted," I said. "Though it makes me wonder what's worth guarding in an abandoned building scheduled for demolition."

Powell didn't respond, but his eyes told me everything I needed to know. The factory was important.

"Enjoy the rest of your evening, Mr. Starke," he said finally. "And consider what I've said."

I left the conference room and headed back toward the ballroom, my mind racing. Within the span of thirty minutes, I'd been warned off by both Harmon and Powell. Lucan had noticed me, too. Three of our primary suspects, all reacting to the mere mention of Michael Reynolds.

They were scared.

Back in the ballroom, Harmon was concluding his speech to enthusiastic applause. I caught my father's eye across the room;

he raised an eyebrow in silent question. I gave a slight nod, indicating I'd gotten what I came for.

As the formal program ended and people began to mingle, I slipped out a side exit, avoiding both Harmon and Powell. Outside, I spotted the black Suburban TJ had mentioned parked with a clear view of the main entrance.

I texted TJ: "Heading back. Factory visit tonight. Have Tim ready with satellite surveillance."

Their warnings had only confirmed what I already suspected. Michael Reynolds was buried at that factory, and they were desperate to keep that secret hidden. With the demolition scheduled for Monday, I had limited time to find the evidence.

Eleanor Reynolds deserved answers. And tonight, I was going to get them—one way or another.

CHAPTER 6

Hallowed Ground

BY THE TIME I GOT BACK TO MY OFFICE, I'D ALREADY BEEN HOME and changed out of the monkey suit and back into my working clothes—jeans, T, and leather jacket. My MP9 was holstered in a shoulder rig under my left arm with two spare mags on my belt, and I'd added my expandable ASP Talon baton to my belt. After the not-so-subtle warnings from Harmon and Powell, I wasn't taking any chances.

Tim and TJ were waiting for me in the conference room, a satellite image of the abandoned CMI factory displayed on the large monitor.

"Powell Protection Services has two guard rotations," Tim explained, pointing to the screen. "They patrol the perimeter every two hours, with the last patrol at midnight. The fence is eight feet high with razor wire, but there's no electronic surveillance beyond the main gate."

"What about inside the building?" I asked.

"No signs of active security systems. The power was disconnected years ago." Tim switched to a blueprint of the factory. "This is the northwest section where they reinforced the floor." He indicated a rectangular area about twenty by thirty feet. "According to the renovation permits, they poured a new concrete slab eighteen inches thick—way more than needed for standard machinery."

"What was in that part of the factory?"

"Originally, it was part of the employee lounge and locker area. The 1999 renovation plans listed it as 'specialized storage.'"

"Specialized storage that required eighteen inches of reinforced concrete," I mused. "Convenient."

TJ looked concerned. "Even if you get past the guards, how do you plan to check under that concrete?"

I patted my jacket pocket. "I borrowed a specialized microphone from a forensic archaeologist friend of mine. It can detect density differences and void spaces beneath concrete. If there's a body down there, this should pick it up."

"And if it does?" TJ asked.

"Then I call Kate Gazzara and get her to bring in the crime scene unit."

Tim adjusted his glasses. "The demolition company has already moved equipment onto the site. Bulldozers, excavators, the works. They're serious about starting Monday morning."

"Which means we have exactly one shot at this." I studied the satellite image again. "When's the next guard patrol?"

Tim checked his watch. "They should be making their 10 p.m. round now. That gives you almost two hours before they circle back."

"Perfect." I pulled on my black leather gloves. "I'll approach from the river side. Less chance of being spotted."

"I've set up a surveillance feed from the nearest traffic camera," Tim said, switching to another screen showing a distant view of the factory entrance. "It's not close enough to see the building itself, but I'll be able to warn you if any vehicles approach."

"Good. TJ, I want you at the old boat launch half a mile downstream. If I need a quick exit, that's where I'll head."

TJ nodded. "I'll be there."

I checked my equipment one last time—flashlight, microphone, digital camera, lock picks, and my phone with a specialized app Tim had designed for secure communications. Plus my MP9. I hoped I wouldn't need it, but Powell's warning about trespassing being "unhealthy" suggested they might have more than regular security guards watching the place.

"I'll head out now. Keep the comm line open."

Tim handed me a small earpiece. "This will keep your hands free. The mic is sensitive enough to pick up even a whisper."

As I turned to leave, TJ caught my arm. "Watch yourself, Harry. These people have already killed once to protect their secret."

"I'm counting on that," I replied. "It means there's something there worth finding."

THE ABANDONED CMI factory loomed like a dark monolith against the night sky. Located on the outskirts of town near the Tennessee River, the massive concrete structure had once employed hundreds of workers. Now it stood empty, surrounded by overgrown parking lots and a recently installed perimeter fence.

I parked my Maxima a quarter mile away in the lot of a shuttered gas station and approached on foot, keeping to the shadows. The night was clear and cool, with enough moonlight to see by once my eyes adjusted. I skirted the main road, cutting through a wooded area that ran along the river's edge until I reached the back of the property.

"I'm at the south fence line," I murmured into my comm. "Any movement on the cameras?"

"All clear," Tim's voice came through the earpiece. "A guard vehicle left the main gate fifteen minutes ago. Next patrol in about an hour and forty-five minutes."

The fence was as Tim had described: eight feet high with razor wire atop. I took a pair of heavy-duty wire cutters from my jacket and made a neat incision about two feet up from the ground, then cut a small opening, just big enough to crawl through. The fence was too obvious to climb; if I needed to make a quick exit, I wanted a discreet way out.

Once inside the perimeter, I moved quickly across the open ground to the shadow of the building. The factory had few windows, most of them broken or boarded up. I found a service entrance on the south side; the door secured with a heavy padlock.

Three minutes with my lock picks, and I was in.

The interior was pitch black. I switched on my flashlight, keeping the beam low and shielded. The air was thick with the smell of dust, mildew, and decaying industrial materials. My footsteps echoed on the concrete floor as I made my way through what had once been the production area.

"I'm inside," I whispered. "Heading toward the northwest section."

"Copy that," Tim replied. "It's still all clear outside."

According to the blueprints, the reinforced area was past the main production floor, near what had been the employee facilities. I moved carefully, avoiding debris and watching for signs of recent activity.

As I approached the northwest corner, I noticed something odd. While most of the factory was thick with dust and cobwebs, this section appeared cleaner. The floor had been swept recently.

"Someone's been here," I murmured.

"Recently?" TJ's voice asked through the comm.

"Within the last few days, by the look of it." I swept my

flashlight across the area. "They've cleared a path to the rein-forced section."

I reached the area indicated on Tim's blueprints. The concrete here was visibly newer than the surrounding floor, a slightly different shade of gray, with none of the cracks and stains that marked the older sections. The rectangular area was exactly as Tim had described, about twenty by thirty feet.

I knelt down and examined the edge where the new concrete met the old. The seam was nearly perfect, but there was a subtle difference in height—the newer section was about a quarter-inch higher.

"I found it," I whispered, removing the specialized micro-phone from my pocket. "Beginning scan now."

The device was about the size of a small tablet, with a sensi-tive microphone and ground-penetrating radar capabilities. I moved it slowly across the surface of the concrete, watching the display for any anomalies.

"Anything?" Tim asked after a few minutes.

"Density is consistent so far," I replied, continuing the scan. "Wait... I've got something."

Near the center of the reinforced area, the device detected a significant anomaly: a void space approximately six feet long by two and a half feet wide, about four feet beneath the surface.

"I'm picking up what could be a burial site," I said, marking the spot with a piece of chalk from my pocket. "The size and depth are consistent with a human body."

"Can you get a visual confirmation?" TJ asked.

"Not without breaking through the concrete." I took several photos of the area and the microphone's display. "But this is enough for Kate to get a warrant."

I continued scanning the entire reinforced section, finding no other anomalies. Whatever was buried there, it was isolated to that single location.

As I was finishing the scan, Tim's urgent voice came

through the comm. "Harry, we've got a vehicle approaching the main gate. Black SUV, no headlights."

My pulse quickened. "Powell Security?"

"Can't tell, but it's definitely not a regular patrol. They're early."

I quickly packed up the microphone and erased the chalk mark with my foot. "I'm on my way out."

"Wait," Tim said. "They're not entering. They've stopped at the gate, like they're waiting for something."

I moved to a boarded-up window, finding a crack to peer through. In the distance, I could see headlights approaching along the main road.

"We've got company," I whispered. "Multiple vehicles."

Through my earpiece, I heard TJ curse softly. "Get out of there, Harry."

"Not yet." I needed to know who was visiting an abandoned factory at nearly midnight.

The new vehicles—I counted three sets of headlights—pulled up to the main gate. The black SUV moved forward, and someone got out to unlock the gate.

"Can you ID any of the vehicles?" I asked Tim.

"Working on it... The lead car is a black Mercedes S-Class. The others look like high-end SUVs, possibly Escalades."

Victor Harmon drove a black Mercedes S-Class. I'd seen it at the Chamber dinner earlier. This couldn't be a coincidence.

"I think our friends are paying a late-night visit to check on their secret," I murmured.

"All the more reason for you to get out now," TJ urged.

He was right. If Harmon and his associates were here, they might be planning to move whatever—or whoever—was buried under that concrete before the demolition crews arrived.

"I'm moving," I said, heading back toward the service entrance. "Keep me posted on their position."

"They're through the gate," Tim reported. "Heading toward the main entrance. Four vehicles total."

I reached the service door and eased it open a crack, peering out. The vehicles were now parked in front of the factory, headlights illuminating the main entrance about a hundred yards from my position.

"I count eight individuals," Tim said, apparently having accessed another camera feed. "Four appear to be security personnel."

"Can you identify the others?"

"Resolution isn't great, but I'm reasonably sure Harmon is one of them. Possibly Lucan too, based on height and build."

I had to get out now, before they spread out and secured the building. I slipped through the service door and hugged the shadows along the side of the factory, moving away from the vehicles and toward my exit point in the fence.

I was halfway there when a beam of light swept across the ground ahead of me. Someone with a flashlight was checking the perimeter.

I froze, pressing myself against the wall of the factory. The security guard was moving methodically along the fence line, his light sweeping back and forth. He hadn't spotted my cut section yet, but he would soon.

"I've got a guard between me and my exit," I whispered into the comm.

"Can you find another way out?" TJ asked.

"Working on it."

The guard was now only about thirty yards from my position, still moving toward my escape route. I needed a distraction.

Reaching into my pocket, I found a small metal object—a heavy-duty office stapler I'd noticed on a desk inside the factory and pocketed as a potential tool. I took careful aim and threw it as far as I could toward the opposite side of the property.

The stapler landed with a satisfying clatter among some metal debris. The guard immediately swung his flashlight in that direction.

"What was that?" he called out, reaching for what I assumed was a radio on his belt.

It was now or never. While his attention was diverted, I sprinted toward my cut in the fence, staying low.

"Movement on the east side," the guard was saying into his radio. "Requesting backup."

I reached the fence and dropped to my stomach, wiggling through the gap I'd created earlier. As I cleared the fence, I heard voices and saw flashlight beams converging on the area where I'd thrown the stapler.

"I'm clear of the fence," I whispered. "Moving toward the extraction point."

"Harry," Tim's voice was urgent in my ear. "One of the SUVs is circling the property. They might be cutting off your escape route."

I quickened my pace, keeping to the tree line that ran between the factory and the river. The boat launch where TJ was waiting was still a quarter mile downstream.

Behind me, I heard shouting. They'd discovered the cut fence.

"They know someone was inside," I told Tim. "How's my path to the boat launch?"

"SUV has stopped at the access road that leads to the launch. They've blocked it."

"Damn." I needed an alternative. "TJ, can you move upstream? There's a drainage culvert about a hundred yards north of my position."

"On my way," TJ replied.

I changed direction, moving north along the river while

staying under cover of the trees. The voices behind me grew more distant, but I knew they'd be organizing a search pattern. Powell's security people were professionals.

The drainage culvert appeared ahead—a large concrete pipe about four feet in diameter that emptied stormwater into the river. It was dry now, and large enough for me to enter in a crouch.

"I'm at the culvert," I whispered. "Any sign of pursuit?"

"They've split up," Tim reported. "Four men heading toward your last known position, two circling north. They're using thermal imaging."

That complicated things. Thermal cameras would pick up my body heat even in the darkness.

I ducked into the culvert, moving about twenty feet in. The concrete would mask my heat signature temporarily, but I couldn't stay here long.

"TJ, what's your status?" I whispered tersely.

"I'm approaching the river bank near the culvert," he replied, his voice low. "I can see flashlights moving along the fence line."

"I'll need to make a water exit. Can you get close enough to the culvert outlet without being seen?"

"Already there," TJ said. "The boat's secured about ten feet offshore."

"On my way."

I moved through the culvert toward the river end. As I neared the outlet, I could see TJ's silhouette against the moonlit water, crouched by the riverbank.

"There are guards moving your way," Tim warned. "Less than a hundred yards north and closing."

I reached the end of the culvert. The drop to the water was about six feet. TJ had positioned a small aluminum boat directly below.

"Jump," he whispered up to me. "I'll catch you."

I didn't hesitate. I lowered myself from the culvert opening and dropped, landing awkwardly in the boat with a muffled thud. TJ steadied the craft, then pushed off from the bank, using a paddle to guide us silently into the current.

As we drifted away from the shore, I saw flashlight beams converging on the culvert. We'd gotten out just in time.

"We're clear," I murmured into the comm. "Heading downstream."

"I'll meet you at the secondary extraction point," Tim replied. "The road below the old railway bridge."

Once we were well into the river's flow, TJ started the small outboard motor, keeping it at its lowest setting to minimize noise. We moved downstream, staying close to the opposite bank from the factory.

"Did you find what you were looking for?" TJ asked, his weathered face barely visible in the moonlight.

"I think Michael Reynolds is buried under that reinforced concrete," I replied. "And based on tonight's visitors, they're worried about what the demolition might uncover."

TJ nodded grimly. "So, what's the next move?"

"We need to get Kate involved officially. The evidence I gathered tonight should be enough for a warrant to halt the demolition and examine that concrete slab."

"You think they'll move the body before Monday?"

I considered this. "They might try, but breaking up and removing that much concrete without heavy equipment would be challenging. My guess is they're discussing options."

"Options like making sure you don't live to tell anyone what you found?"

"That's certainly on the table." I checked my phone. It was just past midnight. "First thing in the morning, I'm meeting with Kate."

We reached the extraction point fifteen minutes later. Tim

was waiting with my car, his expression a mixture of relief and excitement.

"That was close," he said as we approached. "The entire property is swarming with security now. They've called in additional personnel."

"Did you get any clear images of who was there?" I asked.

Tim handed me his tablet. "See for yourself."

The images were grainy, captured from a distance, but recognizable. Victor Harmon, State Senator James Lucan, and Raymond Powell all gathered outside the factory's main entrance. There was a fourth man with them I didn't recognize.

"Who's that?" I pointed to the unknown figure.

"Martin Greene," Tim replied. "Current CEO of CMI. I ran facial recognition to confirm."

All four of our primary suspects, meeting at midnight at an abandoned factory scheduled for demolition. If I'd had any doubts about their involvement in Reynolds' disappearance, they were gone now.

"We need to move fast," I said, getting into my car. "They know someone was inside the factory tonight. They'll be working on damage control."

"What can they do... I mean what do you think they'll do?" TJ asked.

"Either speed up the demolition or try to extract whatever's buried there themselves." I started the engine. "Either way, we're running out of time."

As we pulled away, I glanced back at the distant factory, barely visible in the moonlight. After fifteen years, Michael Reynolds might finally be found. The question was whether we'd be able to gather enough evidence to bring his killers to justice before they erased all traces of their crime.

Eleanor Reynolds deserved answers. And now, I was certain I knew where to find them.

CHAPTER 7

The Security Chief

I was at Kate Gazzara's desk in the Chattanooga PD by 7:30 the next morning, running on two hours of sleep and far too much coffee. Kate looked as fresh as ever despite the early hour, her blonde hair pulled back in a neat ponytail, her sharp eyes examining the photographs and data I'd gathered the night before.

"Let me get this straight," she said, tapping the screen showing the microphone readings. "You think Michael Reynolds is buried under eighteen inches of concrete in an abandoned factory that's scheduled for demolition on Monday?"

"I don't think. I know." I pointed to the anomaly the device had detected. "That's a human-sized void space four feet below the surface. And if you need more convincing, Harmon, Lucan, Powell, and Greene all showed up at midnight for an emergency meeting after I confronted Harmon at the Chamber dinner."

Kate leaned back in her chair, arms crossed. "Which you know, because you were trespassing on private property."

"I prefer 'conducting a preliminary investigation,'" I replied with a hint of a smile.

She wasn't amused. "Harry, you know I can't get a warrant based on evidence obtained illegally."

"You don't need to mention how I got it. Anonymous tip. Confidential informant. Whatever works."

"That's not how this works, and you know it." She sighed, rubbing her temples. "Even if I wanted to help—which I do—Judge Strange would laugh me out of his chambers if I requested a warrant to halt a scheduled demolition based on an 'anonymous tip' about a fifteen-year-old missing person."

"Then we need more evidence," I said. "Something obtained legally that corroborates what I found."

"Such as?"

I considered our options. "What about the renovation permits? The ones showing they reinforced that specific section of flooring right before closing the factory? That's a matter of public record."

"It's suspicious, but not enough by itself." Kate tapped her pen against her desk. "We need someone to talk. Someone who was there."

An idea formed in my mind. "Raymond Powell."

"The security guy? Why would he talk?"

"Because he's the weak link. He handled the physical aspect —disposing of the body—but I doubt he was part of the financial scheme. He was muscle, brought in to clean up their mess."

Kate considered this. "Even if you're right, why would he implicate himself in a murder?"

"Because he might face a worse alternative." I stood up. "Let me talk to him again. Legally, this time. On the record."

"And say what? 'Hey, did you help bury a body fifteen years ago?'"

"Something like that." I checked my watch. "Powell Protection Services opens at nine. I can be there when the doors unlock."

Kate shook her head. "This is thin, Harry. Really thin."

"But you'll try for that warrant if I get something concrete?"

"If—and that's a big if—you get actionable evidence through legal means, yes, I'll take it to the judge." She fixed me with a stern look. "But no more breaking and entering, no threats, no bullying. By the book, or I walk."

"Scout's honor," I said, heading for the door.

"You were never a Scout," she called after me.

I turned, grinning. "How do you know? I could have been an Eagle Scout."

"You got kicked out of Sunday school," she said. "Somehow I doubt the Boy Scouts were more tolerant."

She wasn't wrong.

POWELL PROTECTION SERVICES occupied a modern three-story building in one of Chattanooga's newer office parks. The glass and steel structure projected exactly the image Raymond Powell wanted—sleek, professional, and intimidating. The company logo, a stylized shield, was emblazoned above the entrance in brushed metal.

I pulled into the visitor parking lot at 8:55, just as employees were arriving for the day. My plan was simple: confront Powell directly, gauge his reaction, and see if he might be willing to save himself by turning on the others.

The lobby was all polished marble and indirect lighting, with a security desk manned by a young man in a crisp uniform who looked like he'd just graduated from the police academy.

"I need to see Raymond Powell," I said, handing him one of my business cards.

"Do you have an appointment, sir?" His tone was courteous, but firm.

"No, but he'll want to speak with me. Tell him Harry Starke is here about last night's incident at the factory."

The guard's expression didn't change, but I noticed his posture stiffen slightly at the mention of the factory. He picked up his phone and spoke quietly into it, his eyes never leaving me.

After a moment, he replaced the receiver. "Mr. Powell will see you. Third floor, end of the hallway. Someone will meet you at the elevator."

As I crossed the lobby toward the elevators, I was aware of cameras tracking my movement. Powell was watching, assessing, deciding how to handle me. Good. I wanted him off balance.

The elevator opened on the third floor to reveal a burly man in a tailored suit—clearly security, not administrative staff. He had the blank expression and alert eyes of former military, probably special forces based on the way he carried himself.

"This way, Mr. Starke," he said, leading me down a hallway lined with photographs of Powell with various dignitaries and clients. The message was clear: Raymond Powell had connections, influence, and resources.

The security man stopped at a set of double doors at the end of the hall, knocked once, then opened them without waiting for a response.

Raymond Powell's office was exactly what I expected— large, impeccably furnished, with views of Lookout Mountain through floor-to-ceiling windows. Powell himself stood behind a massive mahogany desk, his stocky frame outlined against the morning light.

"Mr. Starke," he said, his voice deliberately neutral. "I understand you want to see me about last night's... incident."

The security man closed the doors, leaving us alone. I noticed he remained just outside, visible through the frosted glass panels.

"Busy night," I commented, approaching the desk but not sitting. "Midnight meetings at abandoned factories. Not usual business hours."

Powell's expression didn't change. "We had a security breach at a client's property. I was called to assess the situation."

"The client being Victor Harmon? Or perhaps State Senator Lucan?"

"I don't discuss my client list." Powell folded his arms across his chest. "What do you want, Starke?"

I decided to go straight for the jugular. "I know Michael Reynolds is buried under the reinforced concrete in the northwest corner of that factory. I have the sonic images to prove it."

A flicker of something—surprise, concern, calculation—crossed Powell's face before he regained control. "That's a serious accusation."

"It's not an accusation, it's a fact. And here's another fact: the demolition scheduled for Monday will uncover his remains whether you want it to or not."

Powell walked to a cabinet, removed a crystal decanter, and poured himself a measure of amber liquid despite the early hour. He didn't offer me any.

"You seem very certain of your... theory," he said, taking a sip.

"Certain enough that Detective Gazzara is preparing a warrant to halt the demolition and examine that concrete slab." It wasn't precisely true, but Powell didn't need to know that.

"On what grounds?"

"Evidence obtained during a legal investigation into a cold missing persons case." I held his gaze. "Including statements from witnesses who saw unusual activity at the factory the night Reynolds disappeared."

That was a complete bluff, but I watched Powell carefully, looking for a reaction. His expression remained controlled, but his right hand tightened momentarily around his glass.

"These alleged witnesses have remained silent for fifteen years?"

"Some people's consciences catch up with them, eventually." I said, as I moved closer to his desk. "Others decide to protect themselves when they see the writing on the wall."

Powell set his glass down carefully. "Am I supposed to be one of these people with a guilty conscience?"

"I think you're a pragmatist, Mr. Powell. A businessman. And right now, your business interests are at risk."

"Is that a threat?"

"An observation. Three of your biggest clients—Harmon, Lucan, and Greene—are about to face murder charges. The scandal will tank your company. Your reputation for discretion and security will be worthless."

Powell's eyes narrowed. "You're reaching, Starke. Way beyond your grasp."

"Am I?" I leaned forward, palms on his desk. "Let me tell you how I see it. Michael Reynolds discovered financial fraud at CMI—millions siphoned off by Harmon, Lawson, and Lucan. He confronted them, threatened to expose them. It got heated. Someone—probably Lucan—struck him, killed him, maybe it was an accidentally, maybe not."

Powell remained still, his face unreadable.

"That's where you came in," I continued. "They needed someone to handle the mess. You arranged for the security systems to 'malfunction' that weekend. You helped dispose of the body in the most secure location available—under a new concrete floor in a section of the factory scheduled to be mothballed."

"A fascinating story," Powell said flatly. "But pure speculation."

"Then there's the matter of the airport footage—also mysteriously corrupted. Reynolds' car appearing in the long-term lot with no record of who parked it there. The detective pressured to close the case. All very neat. Professional." I straightened up. "Your work, I assume?"

Powell moved to the window, gazing out at the mountain. "I'm a security consultant, Mr. Starke. I protect my clients from threats. That's all."

"And now you're the threat, Raymond. Because you know where all the bodies are buried—literally."

He turned to face me. "What exactly do you want?"

"The truth. For Eleanor Reynolds, who's dying and deserves to know what happened to her son."

"And if I were to hypothetically know something about this case, what would be my incentive to share it?"

Here it was—the opening I'd been waiting for. He hadn't denied anything.

"Simple. When this breaks—and it will break, with or without your help—someone's going to take the fall. Right now, that's likely to be you. The muscle. The guy who handled the dirty work."

Powell scoffed. "You think I'd be the scapegoat?"

"Harmon's a respected businessman with political connections," I said. "Lucan's a state senator with gubernatorial ambitions. Greene runs one of Chattanooga's largest companies. Who do you think they'll throw under the bus when the body is found?"

Uncertainty flashed in Powell's eyes. I pressed my advantage.

"But if you come forward first, provide details only the perpetrator would know... well, the DA has been known to be generous with cooperating witnesses."

Powell returned to his desk, sat down heavily. "You're asking me to confess to a murder."

"I'm offering you a chance to get ahead of what's coming. The first one to talk gets the deal." I pulled out my phone, set it on his desk. "One call to Detective Gazzara, and you can start the process. Voluntary statement. Full cooperation."

He stared at the phone, his internal calculation visible in the tightening of his jaw, the way his eyes flickered between the phone and the door.

"And if I were to... cooperate... what guarantees would I have?"

"I'm sure the DA would consider a reduced charge. Accessory after the fact, maybe. With your military record, first offense... you might get out while you're still young enough to enjoy life."

Powell leaned back in his chair, his face now a mask of professional detachment. "A tempting scenario, Mr. Starke. But entirely hypothetical, of course."

"Of course." I wrote Kate's number on the back of one of my cards, put it on his desk, and picked up my phone. "Think about it," I said. "The demolition is Monday morning. By noon, Michael Reynolds will be found one way or another. The only question is whether you're ahead of the story or buried by it."

I turned to leave, then paused at the door. "One more thing —those regular payments you've been receiving from Harmon, Lucan, and Greene over the years? We found them. All neatly channeled through shell companies, but traceable. Looks an awful lot like ongoing blackmail to me."

Powell's expression hardened. "Your computer guy should be careful where he points that digital microscope. Some systems bite back."

"He's very good at what he does. And he's made copies. Lots of copies." I opened the door. "You have until five o'clock. After that, I take everything to Gazzara, and your leverage is gone."

The security man outside looked to Powell for instructions, but Powell just waved him off. As I walked past, I noticed the gold Breitling Bentley Chronograph on the man's wrist—identical to my own watch. Powell paid his people well.

In the elevator descending to the lobby, I reviewed the confrontation. Powell hadn't denied anything. More importantly, he'd contemplated the deal, which meant he was at least considering betraying his co-conspirators.

As I crossed the lobby, I glanced back at the security cameras. Powell would be watching, weighing his options, calculating the odds. His entire career had been built on risk assessment and threat management. The question was whether he would recognize that his former clients had now become his greatest threat.

Outside in the parking lot, I called TJ.

"How'd it go?" he asked.

"He's thinking about it. I gave him until five o'clock."

"You think he'll talk?"

"Maybe." I got into my car, started the engine. "He's a survivor. If he believes turning on the others is his best chance to save himself, he'll do it."

"And if he doesn't?"

"Then we move to Plan B." I pulled out of the parking lot. "Meet me at the office. We need to prepare for both possibilities."

As I drove away, I checked my rearview mirror. A black sedan was pulling out of the Powell Protection Services lot, following at a discreet distance. Either Powell was having me followed again, or he was on the move himself.

Either way, the game was now fully in play. The only question was who would make the next move—and whether it would be the one I'd planned for.

CHAPTER 8

Political Connections

BACK AT THE OFFICE, I FOUND TIM IN FRONT OF HIS ARRAY OF screens, but with an unusual look of concern on his young face.

"What's wrong?" I asked, dropping into the chair beside his desk.

"Someone's been probing our firewalls since 6 AM," he said, pointing to a screen filled with code I couldn't begin to comprehend. "Sophisticated attacks. Professional-grade stuff."

"Powell?"

Tim shook his head. "Powell Protection Services uses a cybersecurity contractor called Nexus Digital. These attacks are coming from a different source—a firm called Blackridge Security. They specialize in digital counterintelligence."

"Can they get in?"

"Not likely. I've set up multiple defense layers and honey-pots to distract them." A hint of professional pride crept into his voice. "But they're persistent. And well-funded."

"Who uses Blackridge?" I asked, though I had a suspicion.

Tim pulled up another window. "Several major corporations, including..." He paused for dramatic effect. "The office of State Senator James Lucan."

"Lucan's trying to find out what we know."

"And what we can prove." Tim said as he spun in his chair to face me. "I managed to download a significant portion of the CMI archives before they completed their purge, but the most crucial files from 2002 were already gone. Whatever was in the 'Reynolds Problem' file, they deleted it thoroughly."

"So what were you able to salvage?" I asked.

"Financial records showing the pattern of embezzlement we already suspected," he replied, then continued. "Email headers—though not the emails themselves—showing communications between Harmon, Lawson,, and Lucan intensified significantly the week Reynolds disappeared. And—" Tim pulled up a spreadsheet that looked like financial transactions. "Records of substantial payments from Harmon Capital to Lucan's first campaign fund. Three hundred thousand dollars, channeled through various PACs and donors to hide the source."

"Campaign finance violations," I noted. "Serious, but not murder."

"No, but it establishes the relationship between Harmon and Lucan beyond their CMI connection. And there's more." Tim switched to another screen. "After I found those payments, I ran a search for similar patterns involving the other suspects. Look at this."

The screen showed property records for a lake house in North Georgia.

"Who owns it?" I asked.

"On paper, a shell company called Mountain Crest Holdings. But the beneficial owner is Diane Lawson. She purchased it in December 2010 for $1.2 million. All cash, no mortgage."

"Let me guess; another windfall that appeared after Reynolds disappeared."

"Exactly. But here's the interesting part." Tim zoomed in on a section of the record. "Look who signed as the notary on the transaction."

I leaned closer. "James Lucan."

"Before he was Senator Lucan. He was still CMI's legal counsel at the time."

"So Lucan facilitated a major purchase for Lawson using money that likely came from the embezzlement scheme." I considered the implications. "He's more involved than we thought."

"That's not all." Tim pulled up a calendar. "Senator Lucan has a fundraiser scheduled tonight at the Hunter Museum of American Art. All of Chattanooga's power players will be there."

"Including Harmon, no doubt."

"He's on the host committee."

An idea formed in my mind. "Can you get me in?"

Tim raised an eyebrow. "To a $1,000-a-plate fundraiser for a state senator?"

"You're the genius," I said, smiling. "Surely you can add a name to a guest list."

He grinned. "I can do better than that. Give me an hour."

I left Tim to his digital wizardry and found TJ in the conference room, still analyzing the journal entries from Michael Reynolds.

"Find anything new?" I asked.

TJ looked up from his work. "Maybe. There's a pattern to the financial discrepancies Reynolds identified. They weren't random. They were targeted at specific projects—government contracts, primarily."

"CMI had government contracts?"

"Military components, mostly. Nothing classified, but lucrative. The scheme seems to have involved inflating costs, then pocketing the difference."

"Which would make it federal fraud," I mused. "Defrauding the government carries stiffer penalties than ordinary embezzlement."

"And longer statutes of limitation," TJ added. "Some federal fraud charges can be brought up to ten years after the fact."

"So even fifteen years later, Lucan would still have good reason to keep this buried," I said as I sat across from TJ. "Especially with his political ambitions."

TJ nodded. "Word is he's planning a run for governor next year."

"Hard to campaign from a federal prison." I tapped the journal. "Any mention of these government contracts specifically?"

"Just project codes and dollar amounts." TJ pushed a notepad toward me. "I cross-referenced them with public contract records. Three Department of Defense contracts between 2008 and 2010, totaling just over twenty million dollars."

"And how much was skimmed?"

"Based on Reynolds' findings from 2002, I'd say at least four million. Possibly more."

My phone buzzed with a text from Tim: "You're in. Black tie. Plus one if needed."

I showed the message to TJ. "Feel like attending a political fundraiser tonight?"

He grimaced. "Last time I wore a tuxedo was my second wedding. Didn't end well."

"You don't have to come. I'll take Jacque."

"Better choice," TJ agreed. "She actually enjoys those things."

I stood to leave. "Keep digging into those government contracts. I want to know exactly what was being manufactured and who the contracting officers were."

"Already on it."

I found Jacque at her desk, handling what appeared to be

routine client calls with her usual efficiency. When she finished, I perched on the edge of her desk.

"How do you feel about attending a political fundraiser tonight?" I asked.

She raised an eyebrow. "For James Lucan? The man you suspect of murder?"

"You've been talking to Tim."

"I talk to everyone." She tilted her head. "What's your angle?"

"I need to observe Lucan and Harmon together, see how they're handling the pressure. And I might need to have a word with the senator himself."

"You think that's wise? Confronting him publicly?"

"Not a confrontation," I said. "Just a conversation. Very civil, very public." I grinned. "I'll even wear a tux."

"Well, in that case." She checked her calendar. "I'll need to reschedule a dinner, but I can make it work. Hunter Museum at seven?"

"Tim's handling the details. And Jacque—dress to impress. We need to blend with the power players."

She gave me a look that said she didn't need fashion advice from me. "I think I can manage," she said, then smiled.

BEFORE HEADING HOME TO CHANGE, I made a detour to visit Eleanor Reynolds at the hospice facility. I found her in the small garden behind the building, seated in a wheelchair, a blanket over her knees despite the warm day. She looked frailer than when I'd first met her, but her eyes were still clear and alert.

"Mr. Starke," she greeted me. "Any news about Michael?"

I sat on a bench beside her wheelchair. "We're making progress. I think I know what happened to him."

Her hands tightened on the arms of her wheelchair. "Tell me."

Gently, I outlined what we'd discovered: the financial fraud at CMI, Michael's discovery of the scheme, and the likelihood that he had confronted those responsible and been killed as a result. I didn't share my suspicion about where his body was buried; that would be too much right now.

She listened silently; her face composed. When I finished, she nodded slowly.

"I always knew it was something like that. Michael had a strong sense of right and wrong. He wouldn't have stayed silent if he found wrongdoing." A single tear slid down her wrinkled cheek. "Do you know who did it?"

"I have strong suspicions. We're gathering evidence."

"Will they be brought to justice?"

I met her gaze directly. "I promise you they will."

She reached out a thin hand and gripped mine with surprising strength. "Thank you, Mr. Starke. Knowing the truth—even a terrible truth—is better than not knowing."

"I should have more information soon. The case is moving quickly now."

"Good. I don't have much time left." She said it matter-of-factly, without self-pity. "My doctor says a few weeks, maybe less."

"I'll make sure you get answers before then."

As I left the hospice, my resolve hardened. Eleanor Reynolds deserved to see her son's killers brought to justice before she died. I would make that happen, one way or another.

AT PRECISELY SEVEN O'CLOCK, I pulled up to the Hunter Museum of American Art in my freshly detailed Maxima. The valet gave the car a dubious look, then shrugged and handed me a ticket. The museum, perched dramatically on a bluff over-looking the Tennessee River, was Chattanooga's premier cultural institution and a favorite venue for high-end fundraisers.

Jacque met me at the entrance, looking stunning in a white cocktail dress that accentuated the coffee color of her skin. She carried a small clutch and wore her hair in an elegant updo that made her look older than her twenty-nine years—exactly the effect we needed.

"You clean up well," she commented, straightening my bow tie.

"So do you." I offered her my arm. "Shall we?"

Inside, the museum's grand atrium had been transformed into a reception area, with white-clothed tables, crystal chandeliers, and a small orchestra playing understated classical music. The city's elite mingled, glasses of champagne in hand, designer gowns and bespoke suits on display.

Tim had done his job well. Our names were on the list, and we were handed programs and directed toward the bar. I scanned the room, quickly locating our targets.

Victor Harmon stood near the center of the room, commanding attention in a perfectly tailored tuxedo, gesturing as he spoke to a group of admirers. State Senator James Lucan worked the crowd like the practiced politician he was, moving from group to group, shaking hands, his camera-ready smile never faltering.

"There's Diane Lawson," Jacque murmured, nodding toward a blonde woman in a blue gown near the windows. "No sign of Powell."

"He's probably still weighing his options," I replied quietly. "Let's mingle. I want to get closer to Lucan without being obvious."

We worked our way through the crowd, accepting champagne from a passing waiter, exchanging pleasantries with strangers who assumed we belonged. My father would have been proud of my networking skills, honed at his insistence during my youth.

As we circled the room, I noticed Martin Greene, the current CEO of CMI, deep in conversation with Harmon. Their body language suggested tension beneath the social veneer.

"Let's get within earshot," I suggested to Jacque.

We positioned ourselves near a display case showing a glass sculpture, angled so we could overhear without being obvious.

"—absolutely cannot move forward with current plans," Greene was saying, his voice low but intense. "The risks are too high now."

"The wheels are already in motion," Harmon replied, smiling for the benefit of onlookers. "Changing course now would only draw more attention."

"You said the situation was contained."

"It is." Harmon's confidence seemed unshakeable. "Our mutual friend is handling final arrangements as we speak."

"And what about Starke?"

I felt Jacque tense beside me.

"A minor irritant," Harmon said dismissively. "Nothing we can't manage."

Greene didn't look convinced. "He was in the factory, Victor. He knows."

"Suspicion isn't proof. By Monday afternoon, there will be nothing to find."

Their conversation was interrupted as Senator Lucan approached, clapping both men on the shoulder with practiced bonhomie.

"Victor! Martin! Glad you could make it." Lucan's politician smile was fixed in place, but his eyes were watchful. "We need to talk. Privately."

The three men moved away, heading toward a side gallery that had been closed off for the event. I caught Jacque's eye and nodded slightly toward the gallery entrance.

"Create a distraction in about two minutes," I murmured.

She nodded, understanding immediately.

I circled the room, eventually positioning myself near the gallery entrance. When I heard Jacque's laugh—louder than normal and impossible to ignore—ring out across the atrium, followed by the sound of breaking glass, I slipped into the side gallery.

The space was dimly lit, with spotlights illuminating paintings on the walls. I could hear voices from around a corner and moved silently in that direction, staying close to the wall.

"—absolutely insane," Lucan was saying, his political persona stripped away, revealing raw anger. "You were supposed to handle this years ago."

"We did handle it," Harmon replied. "No one could have anticipated Starke digging into this now."

"The mother hired him," Greene said. "She's dying."

"I don't care if she's dying," Lucan snapped. "What I care about is that we have a potential disaster on our hands three months before I announce my gubernatorial campaign."

"Powell has the situation under control," Harmon assured him.

"Does he?" Lucan's voice dripped with skepticism. "Because I heard Starke visited him this morning, offering a deal."

There was a moment of silence.

"What kind of deal?" Harmon asked finally.

"The kind where Powell talks and saves himself while throwing us to the wolves." Lucan's voice had dropped to a dangerous whisper. "If he has any evidence—any at all—linking us to Reynolds..."

"He doesn't," Greene insisted. "Everything was handled properly."

"Except for the body being exactly where Starke thinks it is," Lucan retorted. "We need to accelerate the timetable. Get it moved tonight."

"That's not possible," Harmon said. "The equipment—"

"I don't want excuses, I want solutions. If that concrete is broken up during the demolition and Reynolds is found, we're done. All of us."

"Powell has a team ready," Greene said. "But they can't move until after midnight. The area's too visible during the day."

"Make sure they understand the stakes," Lucan said. "Complete removal. Nothing left to find."

"It's being handled," Harmon assured him.

"It better be. I've invested fifteen years in building my political career. I won't let it be destroyed by this."

I heard movement and quickly retreated to the main atrium, rejoining Jacque just as she finished apologizing to a waiter for the broken champagne glass.

"What did you hear?" she asked quietly as we moved away.

"They're planning to remove the body tonight. After midnight."

"Can we stop them?"

"We can try." I checked my watch. "But first, I need to have a word with the senator."

Lucan had emerged from the side gallery, his political mask firmly back in place as he worked the room. I tracked his movement, waiting for the right moment.

It came when he paused near the bar, momentarily alone, as he ordered a drink. I approached casually, positioning myself beside him.

"Bourbon, neat," I told the bartender, then turned to Lucan. "Senator. Harry Starke. We haven't formally met."

His eyes registered recognition, then wariness, but his smile never faltered. "Mr. Starke. I've heard your name mentioned recently."

"I imagine you have." I accepted my bourbon, raised it slightly. "To successful campaigns."

He clinked his glass against mine automatically, political reflexes taking over. "Thank you for your support."

"I haven't decided who I'm supporting yet," I replied. "Depends on... well, several things."

His eyes hardened, though his smile remained fixed. "Such as?"

"Such as how certain situations are resolved. The Michael Reynolds situation, for instance."

To his credit, Lucan didn't flinch. "I'm not familiar with that name."

"No? That's strange, since you were CMI's legal counsel when he disappeared fifteen years ago. And since his name appeared in a file called the 'Reynolds Problem' that was recently purged from CMI's servers."

Lucan took a careful sip of his drink. "Mr. Starke, I dealt with hundreds of legal matters in my career. I can't be expected to remember every name."

"Even when that name is connected to four million dollars in defense contract fraud? The kind of fraud that carries federal charges with a ten-year statute of limitations?"

A muscle twitched in Lucan's jaw. "I think you've misunderstood something fundamental, Mr. Starke. I'm a state senator with powerful friends and a bright political future. You're a private investigator with a reputation for cutting corners."

"True on both counts."

"Then let me give you some friendly advice." His voice dropped, the political veneer cracking to reveal the steel beneath. "Drop this investigation. Whatever you think you know, whatever you think you can prove, it's not worth the consequences."

"Consequences like what happened to Michael Reynolds?"

Lucan's eyes flashed with genuine anger before he

controlled himself. "I do not know what happened to that young man. But I do know what happens to people who make unfounded accusations against public figures. Defamation suits. Counter-investigations. Ruined reputations."

"Is that a threat, Senator?"

"Of course not." He straightened his bow tie. "Now, if you'll excuse me, I have guests to attend to."

As he turned to leave, I said quietly, "One more question, Senator—how do you think the voters will react when they learn their candidate for governor is linked to a fifteen-year-old murder? Especially when the body is found during Monday's factory demolition?"

Lucan froze, then turned back slowly. "There will be nothing found at that factory, Mr. Starke. Nothing at all."

With that, he walked away, his shoulders rigid beneath his expensive tuxedo.

I rejoined Jacque, who had been watching from a discreet distance. "He's rattled," she observed.

"Good. Rattled people make mistakes." I checked my watch again. "We need to get out of here. They're planning to move the body tonight, and I need to make sure that doesn't happen."

We made our exit, retrieving my car from the valet. As we pulled away from the museum, I noticed a black Suburban parked across the street, its engine running.

"We've got company," Jacque noted, glancing in the side mirror.

"Powell's people," I confirmed. "They're not even trying to be subtle anymore."

"What's the play?"

"First, we lose our tail. Then we call Kate Gazzara and set up a stakeout at the factory. If they try to remove Michael Reynolds tonight, we'll be ready to catch them in the act."

I pressed harder on the accelerator, the Maxima's modified

engine responding instantly. The Suburban pulled out behind us, matching our speed.

"Hold on," I told Jacque. "This might get interesting."

The game of cat and mouse had begun. But what our pursuers didn't realize was that sometimes, the mouse had teeth.

CHAPTER 9

Threats and Warnings

AFTER LEAVING THE HUNTER MUSEUM, I CHECKED MY WATCH. IT was 8:45 PM. The 5 PM deadline I'd given Powell had come and gone with no word from the security chief. I wasn't surprised, but I was disappointed. I'd genuinely thought he might be the weak link.

"Powell didn't take the deal," I told Jacque as we navigated through downtown Chattanooga, the black Suburban still trailing us.

"You really expected him to?" she asked.

"I thought he might. Self-preservation is a powerful motivator."

"Maybe he got a better offer," Jacque suggested, glancing at the side mirror. "Our friends are still with us."

"Let's see how committed they are." I made a sudden right turn onto Market Street, then an immediate left into an alley between two office buildings. The Suburban couldn't make the turn in time and shot past the alley.

"They'll circle back," Jacque warned.

"I'm counting on it." I followed the alley to its end, emerging onto Broad Street, then made another quick right. We weaved through downtown, making unpredictable turns, using one-way streets to our advantage.

As we approached the Walnut Street Bridge, I checked the rearview mirror. "I think we lost them."

"Temporarily," Jacque said. "They'll be watching your condo and the office."

"Which is why we're not going to either place." I pulled out my phone and dialed Kate Gazzara's number.

She answered on the third ring. "This better be good, Harry. I'm off duty."

"Remember that factory I told you about? They're planning to move the body tonight. Around midnight."

There was a pause. "And you know this how?"

"I overheard Lucan, Harmon, and Greene discussing it at the fundraiser. They're sending a team to extract everything before the demolition."

"You were at Lucan's fundraiser?" Her voice held a mix of disbelief and resignation.

"Focus, Kate. This is our chance to catch them in the act. But I need official backup. Powell's security people are already trailing me."

Another pause, longer this time. "Meet me at the station in twenty minutes. And Harry—don't do anything stupid before I get there."

"Would I do that?"

"In a heartbeat," she replied, then hung up.

I turned to Jacque. "Change of plans. We need to swing by the office first. I want Tim to set up remote surveillance on the factory perimeter."

"What about Powell's people?" she asked.

"They can't watch every entrance. We'll use the loading dock in the back."

Twenty minutes later, we pulled up to the rear of our office building. As expected, a black sedan was parked across the street from the main entrance, but the rear of the building was clear, so we slipped in through the back door.

Tim was still in his lair, surrounded by his screens. He barely looked up as we entered.

"Powell didn't take the deal," he said before I could speak.

"How do you know?"

"Because at 4:58 PM, he made three calls; one each to Harmon, Lucan, and Greene. Short calls, less than a minute each. Then at 5:05, he sent a text to a number registered to Powell Protection Services with the message: 'Package secure. Standby for retrieval instructions.'"

I raised an eyebrow. "You're monitoring his communications?"

Tim shrugged. "You said to dig deeper. I dug."

"Any idea what the 'package' refers to?"

"Based on the timing and context? Either he's talking about you, or about Reynolds' remains."

"Or both," Jacque suggested.

I nodded. "They're definitely planning to remove the body tonight. I need you to set up remote surveillance on the factory. Any cameras in the area we can access?"

Tim swiveled to another screen. "There's a traffic cam at the intersection nearest the main gate, but it doesn't show the entire property. However—" he pulled up satellite imagery, "—I can re-task a commercial satellite for a thermal sweep of the area."

"You can do that?" I asked, shocked by even the thought of it.

He gave me a look that said I shouldn't ask questions I didn't want answers to. "Give me ten minutes."

While Tim worked his digital magic, I briefed TJ, who had remained at the office analyzing financial records.

"So Powell decided to stick with his people," TJ said, unsurprised. "He must think they have a better chance of containing this than turning state's evidence."

"Or they made him a counter offer he couldn't refuse."

"Either way, we need to move fast." TJ handed me a folder. "I found something interesting in those DOD contracts. The components CMI was manufacturing were guidance systems for drones. Cutting-edge technology at the time."

"Military applications?"

"Initially. But Harmon filed patents on modified versions of the technology right after leaving CMI. Those patents became the foundation of Harmon Capital's first major investment—a tech startup called NaviSys that specialized in civilian drone applications."

"So he didn't just steal money, he stole technology," I said, seeing the bigger picture. "That would definitely be worth killing to protect."

"Especially when NaviSys was acquired by a defense contractor in 2015 for $120 million. Harmon's stake was valued at roughly $40 million."

The pieces were falling into place. Michael Reynolds had stumbled onto something much bigger than simple embezzlement; industrial espionage involving military technology.

Tim called from his office. "Harry, you need to see this."

We gathered around his workstation. One screen showed thermal satellite imagery of the abandoned factory, with several bright spots indicating heat signatures.

"This was taken five minutes ago," Tim explained. "We've got at least four vehicles at the factory already, and what looks like a dozen or so people moving around the site."

"They're not waiting until midnight," I realized. "They're starting now."

"There's more." Tim switched to another screen showing my condo building. "Two men watching your place. And another team at Jacque's apartment."

"What about TJ's place?"

"Clear so far."

I turned to TJ. "They don't know about you yet. That's an advantage."

"What's the play?" he asked.

"I need to meet Kate at the police station. She's our best chance of getting official intervention before they remove all the evidence."

"They're watching the building exits," Jacque reminded me.

"Not all of them." I turned to Tim. "Remember that maintenance tunnel we found during the building renovation last year? The one that connects to the parking garage for the building next door?"

Tim nodded. "It hasn't been sealed yet. Construction's still ongoing."

"That's our exit." I checked my weapon, making sure it was fully loaded. "Jacque, you stay here. Coordinate with Tim on the surveillance. TJ, I want you to head to the factory in your car. Keep your distance, but be ready to document anything you see."

"What about Powell's people?" Jacque asked.

"They're expecting me to leave in my car. They won't be looking for TJ or for someone leaving through the building next door." I turned to TJ. "Go to the basement. The access panel to the tunnel is behind the electrical room."

TJ nodded. "Be careful, Harry. These people are playing for keeps now."

"So am I," I said.

Before leaving, I checked my phone. A text had come in from an unknown number: "Walk away now. Last warning."

I showed it to Jacque. "Looks like they're getting nervous."

"Or desperate," she replied, her expression concerned. "Either way, it makes them dangerous."

"I'll be fine," I said. "Just keep the lines of communications open and alert me to any movement at the factory."

I took the stairs down to the basement, found the access panel to the maintenance tunnel, and made my way through the dusty, cramped space to the adjacent building's parking garage. From there, I took the steps to the street level and walked casually to a coffee shop two blocks away, where I'd arranged for an Uber under a fake name.

Twenty minutes later, I was at the police station, where Kate was waiting impatiently in the parking lot.

"You're late," she said as I approached.

"Had to take precautions. Powell's people are watching my every move."

She frowned. "That's not just routine surveillance. That's stalking, possibly intimidation."

"Tell me about it," I said. "They've escalated from following to threatening." I showed her the text message.

Kate's frown deepened. "This is getting serious, Harry. These aren't just wealthy businessmen covering up financial crimes. They're willing to cross lines."

"They crossed the ultimate line fifteen years ago when they killed Michael Reynolds," I reminded her. "Everything since has been about covering that up."

She led me inside to a small conference room where two other detectives were waiting. I recognized one of them—Mike Delaney, a veteran homicide detective who'd worked with Kate on several cases. The other was younger, with the alert posture of former military.

"This is Detective Delaney," Kate introduced, "and Detective Wilson. They'll be helping us tonight."

I shook their hands. "What's the plan?"

"That depends on what you can give us," Kate said. "I need something concrete, Harry. Something that justifies a late-night operation at a private property."

I laid out everything we'd discovered—the financial fraud, the technology theft, the reinforced concrete section in the factory, the microphone readings indicating a human-sized void, and most importantly, the overheard conversation at the fundraiser explicitly mentioning plans to remove what was buried there.

"The satellite thermal imaging confirms there's activity at the factory right now," I concluded. "They're not waiting until midnight. They're moving now."

Delaney looked skeptical. "All circumstantial. No judge would issue a warrant based on this."

"What about the defense contract fraud?" I countered. "That alone would justify an investigation."

"Different jurisdiction," Kate pointed out. "That would be FBI territory."

"Then call them in," I urged. "But we need to move now. By morning, any evidence will be gone."

Kate exchanged looks with the other detectives, then made a decision. "We'll do a drive-by. If there's visible activity that suggests criminal trespass or unauthorized demolition after hours, we'll have grounds to investigate further."

"That's not enough," I argued. "By the time you establish probable cause, they'll have cleared out."

"It's the best I can do legally, Harry. We need to play this by the book if we want any charges to stick."

I couldn't argue with her logic, but it was frustrating. "Fine. Let's go."

As we headed for the door, my phone buzzed with a text from Tim: "They're moving heavy equipment on site. Looks like they brought in a small excavator and concrete cutting tools."

I showed the message to Kate. "They're bringing in heavy equipment. After business hours, without permits, at a property scheduled for official demolition Monday. That's got to be enough for you to check it out officially."

She nodded reluctantly. "We'll take two cars. You ride with me. Delaney and Wilson will follow."

Ten minutes later, we were approaching the factory from a back road, lights off to avoid early detection. I'd texted TJ our approach, and he confirmed he was in position on the river side of the property with a clear view of the activity.

"There are multiple vehicles inside the fence," he reported. "Security personnel stationed at all entrance points. Heavy equipment moving toward the northwest corner of the building."

"They're not wasting any time," I told Kate.

She parked about a quarter-mile from the main gate, using binoculars to assess the situation. "I count four security personnel at the gate. Armed, wearing Powell Protection uniforms."

"Any sign of Powell himself? Or Harmon, Lucan, Greene?"

"Not visible from this angle."

Delaney and Wilson pulled up behind us, and Kate briefed them. "We've got armed private security guarding a supposedly abandoned property, with unauthorized heavy equipment being operated after hours. That's enough for us to approach and inquire."

"How do you want to play it?" Delaney asked.

"Official capacity. We received a noise complaint from a passing motorist. Standard procedure." Kate turned to me. "You stay in the car, Harry. We can't have a civilian involved in the initial contact."

I didn't like it, but I understood. "Just don't let them stall until they've removed the evidence."

"Trust me." Kate checked her weapon, then spoke into her radio. "Dispatch, this is Lieutenant Gazzara. We're investigating a possible trespassing and unauthorized construction at the old CMI factory on River Road. Request backup units to our location."

"Copy that, Lieutenant. Units en route. ETA fifteen minutes."

Kate nodded to the other detectives. "Let's move."

As they drove toward the main gate in Delaney's unmarked car, my phone buzzed with another text from Tim: "Heat signatures concentrating in the NW corner of the building. They're definitely focusing on the reinforced area."

I forwarded the message to Kate, then settled in to wait. Through the binoculars, I watched as Delaney's car approached the gate. The security personnel immediately moved to block access, hands hovering near their weapons.

Even from this distance, I could see the confrontation growing tense. Delaney and Wilson had exited their vehicle, badges displayed, while Kate appeared to be doing most of the talking. One of the security guards made a call on his radio, looking increasingly agitated.

After what seemed like an eternity but was probably only a few minutes, the gate was reluctantly opened, and the detectives were allowed to drive through. As soon as they were inside, the gate was shut again.

My phone rang—it was TJ.

"They're moving fast," he reported. "I can see through a broken window. They've got concrete cutting equipment running. Some kind of specialized saw."

"Can you see what they're cutting?"

"Not clearly, but based on the position, it has to be the reinforced section you identified."

"Any sign of our primary suspects?" I asked.

"Powell is definitely on site, directing operations. I haven't spotted Harmon, Lucan, or Greene, but there's a black Mercedes parked near the main entrance that matches Harmon's."

"Keep watching. Let me know if anything changes."

I hung up and continued monitoring through the binoculars. Kate and the other detectives had parked near the main entrance and appeared to be in conversation with someone—probably the site supervisor. I could see them gesturing toward the building, likely requesting access to investigate the noise.

My phone buzzed with a text from Tim: "Satellite shows vehicles approaching from the south access road. Three SUVs moving fast."

Reinforcements, but for which side? I checked my watch. The police backup was still at least ten minutes out.

Through the binoculars, I saw the three SUVs pull up to the gate. The security personnel opened it immediately, confirming these were Powell's people. The vehicles drove through and parked near the main entrance.

What happened next made my blood run cold. Several men emerged from the SUVs and surrounded Kate, Delaney, and Wilson. Even from this distance, I could see their postures were threatening.

My phone rang again—this time it was Kate.

"We've got a situation," she said, her voice tense but controlled. "They're refusing access to the building, claiming private property rights and demanding a warrant. Now we've got additional security personnel effectively blocking us from moving."

"That's illegal detention of police officers," I pointed out.

"They're being careful to frame it as 'security protocol' while they contact the property owners. But it's clear they're stalling." She lowered her voice. "Backup is still ten minutes out. If they're removing evidence, we need to act now."

"I'm coming in," I decided.

"No, Harry. That would only escalate—"

I hung up and started the car. If Powell's people were

detaining police officers, they were getting desperate. I couldn't wait for backup.

As I was about to pull out, my phone buzzed with a text from TJ: "They've broken through the concrete. They're removing something wrapped in plastic. Looks like a body bag."

Time had run out. I floored the accelerator, heading not for the main gate but for the section of fence I'd cut the night before. If it hadn't been repaired, I'd have a direct route to the northwest corner of the building.

The car's powerful engine roared as I raced along the perimeter road, headlights off, navigating by moonlight. I spotted the cut section of fence—still open—and aimed directly for it.

The car skidded to a stop, and I jumped out, gun drawn. I could hear the concrete cutting equipment inside the building, the harsh mechanical whine echoing in the night. I moved quickly through the fence opening and approached the factory wall, staying in the shadows.

Through a broken window, I could see exactly what TJ had described—a team of men in work clothes using specialized equipment to cut through the concrete floor. They had already created a large opening, and were in the process of lifting something wrapped in heavy black plastic.

A body. After fifteen years, Michael Reynolds was being moved.

I needed evidence. I pulled out my phone and began recording video of the operation. If they managed to remove the remains before police backup arrived, at least I'd have documentation of what had happened.

As I recorded, I noticed Raymond Powell standing to one side, directing the operation with terse commands. Next to him stood a figure I recognized instantly—Victor Harmon, immaculate in an expensive overcoat despite the dust and grime of the construction site.

I zoomed in on their faces, making sure they were clearly identifiable in the video. I was so focused on capturing the evidence that I didn't notice the security guard until it was too late.

"Drop the phone! Hands where I can see them!"

I turned to find a Powell Protection guard aiming a gun at my head from less than ten feet away. His stance was professional—former military or law enforcement—and his aim was steady.

"I'm unarmed," I lied, keeping my MP9 concealed beneath my jacket. "Just a curious passerby."

"The hell you are." He raised his other hand to his radio. "I've got Starke at the southwest corner. Approaching the target area."

So they knew exactly who I was and had been watching for me. Not surprising, but definitely concerning.

"On your knees," the guard ordered. "Hands behind your head."

I had to stall. Police backup would be arriving soon, and I needed them to find the body before it was removed.

"I'm a licensed private investigator," I said, slowly lowering myself to one knee. "There are police officers at the main gate. Detaining me would be a serious offense."

"The police aren't coming back here," the guard said with a smirk. "They're busy dealing with a trespassing complaint at the front gate. Now both knees, hands behind your head."

As I lowered my other knee to the ground, I heard a sharp crack from somewhere to my left. The guard's expression changed from smug to surprised as he crumpled to the ground, unconscious.

TJ stood behind him, holding what looked like a heavy flashlight. "Figured you could use some help," he said dryly.

"Perfect timing." I got to my feet. "They're removing the body right now. We need to delay them until backup arrives."

"How do you propose we do that? There are at least a dozen men in there, all armed."

I thought quickly. "We don't need to stop them. We just need to document what they're doing and make sure the police see it."

I retrieved my phone, which was still recording, and moved closer to the window. Inside, the workers had fully extracted the body bag from the concrete hole and were preparing to move it to a waiting vehicle.

"I need a distraction," I told TJ. "Something to draw the security personnel from the main gate back here without alerting the extraction team."

TJ nodded. "Fire alarm?"

"Perfect," I said. "Do it."

While I continued filming, TJ moved to a fire alarm pull station near one of the factory's side doors. With a quick tug, the alarm began blaring throughout the building, red lights flashing.

The effect was immediate. The extraction team froze, looking to Powell and Harmon for direction. Powell began shouting orders, pointing toward the exits, while Harmon looked around frantically.

Through the window, I heard Powell's voice: "Keep going! Get it to the truck now!"

The workers resumed their task, carrying the body bag toward a loading dock where a black van waited with its rear doors open.

Inside, I knew Kate and the other detectives would have heard the alarm. It was the opportunity they needed to break away and investigate the rest of the property.

"Help me up," I told TJ, pointing to the broken window. "I need to get inside."

TJ gave me a boost, and I climbed through the window, dropping silently to the factory floor about twenty feet from the extraction team. I stayed in the shadows, continuing to record with my phone as they loaded the body bag into the van.

Harmon was now on his phone, clearly agitated. "I don't care what they're saying! Keep them at the front gate until we're clear!"

Powell approached him. "We need to move now. If that's a real fire, the department will be here in minutes."

"It's not a real fire," Harmon snapped. "It's Starke. He's here somewhere."

Powell drew his weapon. "I'll find him. Get the package out of here."

As Powell began searching the shadows, I retreated toward a row of old manufacturing equipment, keeping my phone trained on the van. I needed clear evidence of the body being removed.

The worker slammed the van's rear doors shut, and the driver started the engine. They were seconds away from driving off with Michael Reynolds' remains.

Suddenly, a spotlight blazed through the loading dock entrance, followed by the unmistakable sound of police sirens.

"CPD! This is Detective Gazzara! Everyone freeze! Hands where we can see them!"

Kate's voice echoed through a bullhorn as patrol cars surrounded the loading area, their lights casting eerie blue and red patterns across the factory interior.

The van driver panicked, gunning the engine and trying to drive through the police blockade. Two patrol cars moved to intercept, forcing the van to swerve and crash into a concrete pillar.

Chaos erupted. Powell's security team scattered, some raising weapons, others fleeing into the shadows. Harmon stood frozen, his face a mask of disbelief as his carefully constructed plan collapsed around him.

I emerged from my hiding place, weapon drawn, and approached Powell from behind. "It's over, Raymond."

He turned, his own weapon still in hand. For a moment, I thought he might try to shoot it out, but something in his eyes changed; a calculation, a realization that the odds had shifted permanently against him.

Slowly, he lowered his gun. "You should have taken the money Harmon offered you to walk away," he said quietly.

"There isn't enough money in the world," I replied.

Police officers swarmed into the building, securing the scene. Kate approached, her expression a mix of professional satisfaction and personal exasperation.

"You couldn't stay in the car, could you?" she asked, though there was no real anger in her voice.

"Would you have?" I retorted.

She shook her head. "The van? That's the body?"

I nodded. "Michael Reynolds, I'm pretty sure. Wrapped in plastic, just extracted from the concrete."

"We've got them," she said, watching as officers handcuffed Harmon and the extraction team. "Dead to rights."

"Not all of them," I pointed out. "Lucan and Greene aren't here."

"We'll get them too." Kate turned to an officer. "Secure that van. Nothing goes in or out without my direct authorization. And someone find me Doc Sheddon. I want him here ASAP."

As the police secured the scene, I found TJ waiting outside the building.

"Hell of a night," he commented.

"And it's not over yet." I checked my phone, finding several missed calls from Tim. I called him back.

"Harry! Thank God. Are you okay?"

"I'm fine. We stopped them. The police have the body and Harmon in custody."

"Lucan just made a call to his private pilot," Tim reported. "He's trying to flee. Filed a flight plan to the Caymans."

"Where is he now?"

"Heading to the executive airport. ETA twenty minutes."

I relayed this information to Kate, who immediately dispatched officers to intercept the senator.

"What about Greene?" I asked Tim.

"No movement yet. Still at his home in Lookout Mountain."

"Keep monitoring. I'll head back to the office once things are wrapped up here."

As I hung up, I watched the medical examiner's van arrive. Doc Sheddon, the short, overweight head of the Hamilton County Forensic Center, emerged, carrying his black case and wadding toward the factory, puffing with exertion.

After fifteen years, Michael Reynolds would finally be properly identified and laid to rest. His mother would get the closure she sought, and the men responsible for his death would face justice.

But the night wasn't over yet. The conspiracy was unraveling, but some threads still needed to be pulled. Lucan was trying to flee, and Greene was still unaccounted for. The next few hours would be critical in making sure all the conspirators were held accountable.

Eleanor Reynolds had hired me to find answers, and I had found them. Now I needed to make sure those answers led to justice.

CHAPTER 10

The Diner Witness

THE NEXT MORNING DAWNED BRIGHT AND CLEAR, A STARK contrast to the chaos of the previous night. I was back at my office by seven, running on black coffee and adrenaline after only a few hours of sleep. The events at the factory had blown the case wide open, but we still needed to solidify the evidence connecting all the conspirators to Michael Reynolds' murder.

Jacque met me at the door with a fresh cup of coffee and the morning's Times Free Press. The front page headline screamed: "PROMINENT BUSINESSMAN ARRESTED IN CONNECTION WITH 15-YEAR-OLD COLD CASE!"

"They didn't waste any time," I commented, taking the paper.

"Kate released a statement around 5 AM," Jacque said. "Kept it vague; just that remains believed to be Michael Reynolds were recovered and Victor Harmon was arrested at the scene. No mention of Lucan yet."

"Did they get him at the airport?"

"They did. Trying to board his private jet with a suitcase full of cash and his passport. He's claiming diplomatic immunity as a state senator."

I snorted. "That's not how it works."

"His lawyers are working every angle." Jacque handed me a folder. "Tim printed this off the police database—" She paused when she saw the look on my face, then smiled and said, "Don't worry. Kate gave him temporary access. The preliminary examination confirms the remains are male, approximately the right age and height for Reynolds. DNA testing is underway, but it will take time."

"What about cause of death?"

"Blunt force trauma to the back of the skull. Doc Sheddon found traces of metal in the wound consistent with a steel pipe or similar object."

Just as I had theorized to Powell. I felt a grim satisfaction that my reconstruction of events had been accurate.

"Any statements from the suspects?"

"Harmon's lawyer issued a 'no comment' and demanded his client's immediate release. Powell is exercising his right to remain silent. Lucan is claiming political persecution and threatening to sue everyone from the arresting officers to the police commissioner."

"And Greene?"

"Disappeared. Didn't come home last night. His wife reported him missing this morning."

That was concerning. "Put Tim on finding him. Bank records, credit cards, phone GPS—whatever it takes."

"Already on it," Jacque assured me. "What's your next move?"

I sipped my coffee, considering our options. "We need to solidify the timeline from the night Reynolds disappeared. We know he confronted Harmon about the financial irregularities, but we need eyewitnesses who saw them together that night."

"After fifteen years?" she said skeptically. "That's a long shot."

"Maybe not." I pulled Michael's journal from my desk drawer. "The last entry mentions meeting Harmon. No location is specified, but earlier entries refer to a place called 'The Usual Spot.' I'm betting that was The Sorbonne."

Jacque raised an eyebrow. "Benny Hinkle's sleazy bar? Doesn't seem like a place a corporate CFO would frequent."

"Perfect for a discreet meeting, though. No one who matters would see them there." I flipped through the journal. "Reynolds also mentions a waitress named Sarah who always remembered his order."

"Sarah who?"

"Just Sarah. But if she worked at The Sorbonne fifteen years ago and is still in the area, Benny will know how to find her."

"And you think she'll remember a specific argument from fifteen years ago?"

"If it involved a man who disappeared the same night? Worth asking." I checked my watch. "The Sorbonne won't open until noon. In the meantime, I want to visit Eleanor Reynolds. She should hear about last night's discovery from me, not the news."

Jacque nodded. "I'll call the hospice and let them know you're coming."

———

ELEANOR REYNOLDS WAS SITTING by the window in her hospice room when I arrived, a newspaper spread on the table beside her. She looked even frailer than before, her skin almost translucent in the morning light, but her eyes brightened when she saw me.

"Mr. Starke," she greeted me, her voice thin but steady. "I was hoping you'd come. The nurses wouldn't tell me anything, but I knew something had happened when I saw the paper."

I sat in the chair beside her. "We found him, Mrs. Reynolds. We found Michael."

She closed her eyes briefly, a mixture of pain and relief crossing her face. "Where?"

"Buried at the old factory where he worked. Under concrete that was poured shortly after he disappeared."

"Was he... did he suffer?" The question every mother dreads asking.

"The medical examiner believes it was quick. A single blow to the head."

She nodded slowly, absorbing this. "And the people responsible?"

"Victor Harmon and Raymond Powell were arrested at the scene last night, caught in the act of trying to remove Michael's body before the factory demolition. State Senator James Lucan was arrested trying to flee the country. Martin Greene is currently missing, but the police are searching for him."

"Lucan." She spoke the name as if testing it. "He was just a lawyer back then, wasn't he? At the company?"

"Yes. He used money from the embezzlement scheme to fund his first political campaign."

"All these years," she murmured. "All these years building their lives, their careers, their fortunes... while my son lay buried under concrete." Her hands trembled slightly as she adjusted the blanket over her knees. "Will they be convicted?"

"The evidence is strong," I assured her. "They were caught in the act of removing the body. And we're still building the case—connecting all the dots from that night."

"Tell me everything," she said. "I want to know exactly what happened to my son."

I hesitated, not wanting to cause her additional pain, but the determination in her eyes convinced me she deserved the full truth. I outlined what we'd discovered—the financial fraud, the technology theft, Michael's discovery of the scheme, and his final confrontation with Harmon that had likely led to his death.

She listened without interruption, her face composed despite the tears that occasionally slipped down her cheeks.

"He always had such a strong sense of right and wrong," she said when I finished. "Even as a little boy. He couldn't bear to see anyone cheated or treated unfairly." A small, sad smile touched her lips. "I used to worry it would make his life difficult. I never imagined it would cost him his life."

"He was brave," I said. "Standing up to powerful people, trying to do the right thing."

"Yes, he was." She reached for a tissue, dabbing at her eyes. "His brother Thomas called this morning. He's flying in today. He's been searching for answers all these years too, you know. He never believed Michael just up and left."

"I'd like to meet him when he arrives."

"Of course." She looked at me with sudden intensity. "Mr. Starke, I need to ask you something, and I want the truth."

"Anything."

"Will I live to see them convicted? To see justice for my son?"

The bluntness of her question caught me off guard, but I owed her honesty. "The legal system moves slowly, Mrs. Reynolds. The trial could be months away."

She nodded, accepting this reality. "Then promise me something. Promise me you won't stop until they've paid for what they did. Even if I'm not here to see it."

"I promise," I said, and meant it. "They won't escape justice."

Our conversation was interrupted by a nurse who came to administer Eleanor's medication. I took my leave, promising to return with any new developments.

As I left the hospice, my resolve hardened. Eleanor

Reynolds was running out of time. I needed to speed up the investigation, find every piece of evidence that would ensure swift justice for her son.

THE SORBONNE LOOKED EVEN MORE depressing in daylight—a squat, windowless building with a neon sign that hadn't worked properly in years. The parking lot was nearly empty when I arrived just after noon, with only a few beat-up cars belonging to the early regulars who treated Benny's watered-down drinks as lunch.

Inside, it took a moment for my eyes to adjust to the dim lighting. The place smelled of stale beer and desperation, with decades of cigarette smoke embedded in every surface despite the smoking ban. A few solitary drinkers hunched over the bar, while Benny himself was stacking glasses behind it.

"Harry Starke," he greeted me without enthusiasm. "Bit early for you, isn't it?"

"I'm not here for a drink, Benny." I approached the bar. "I need some information."

He eyed me suspiciously. Benny Hinkle was a greasy, unshaven slob who inhabited the Sorbonne like some great nocturnal sloth, but he wasn't stupid. He'd survived in this business by knowing when to talk and when to shut up.

"What kind of information?"

"I'm looking for someone who used to work here. A waitress named Sarah. Would have been here about fifteen years ago."

Benny's expression didn't change, but I caught a flicker of recognition in his eyes. "Don't remember anyone by that name."

He was lying. I placed a hundred-dollar bill on the bar. "Try harder."

He glanced at the money but didn't take it. "Lot of wait-resses come and go. Can't be expected to remember all of them."

I added another hundred. "This one might have witnessed something important the night Michael Reynolds disappeared. The case is back in the news—you probably saw the headlines."

Benny's eyes darted to the paper on the end of the bar. "That business with Harmon and the senator? What's that got to do with my place?"

"Reynolds was here the night he disappeared. Met with Harmon. They argued. Sarah might have seen it."

Benny wiped his hands on a towel that looked dirtier than his fingers. "Look, Harry, I run a respectable establishment—"

I couldn't help it—I laughed. "Respectable? The Sorbonne is a boil on Chattanooga's ass, and we both know it. Now, are you going to tell me about Sarah, or do I need to ask the ABC Board to do a surprise inspection?"

The threat of the Alcoholic Beverage Control Board was effective. Benny's face darkened, but he reached for the money.

"Sarah Jenkins. Worked here from 1998 to 2002. Moved on to wait tables at the Waffle House on Shallowford Road for a few years. Last I heard, she was managing a diner out by the airport. Place called The Blue Plate."

"She still in contact with anyone here?"

"Laura might know more. She and Sarah were friendly." He nodded toward a blowsy bottle blonde in a tank top and Daisy Dukes who was wiping down tables across the room.

"Thanks, Benny." I pushed away from the bar. "If the police come asking, you'll tell them the same thing, right?"

"Yeah, yeah." He pocketed the money with a scowl. "Just keep the ABC off my back."

I approached Laura, who eyed me with the wariness of a woman who'd dealt with too many unwanted advances in dive bars.

"Hello, Harry. What can I do for you?" she asked, one hand on her hip.

"I'm looking for Sarah Jenkins. Benny said you might know how to reach her."

"Who's asking?"

"Me. I'm asking. It's about a case from fifteen years ago—might have witnessed something important."

Laura sighed. "Sarah's been through enough crap in her life. She doesn't need old trouble stirred up."

"This is about bringing justice for a murdered young man," I said quietly. "His mother is dying and deserves closure."

Something in my tone must have convinced her. Laura sighed, pulled out her phone, and scrolled through her contacts.

"She's still at The Blue Plate. Works the morning shift, six to two." She gave me a hard look. "She's got a good life now. Husband, kids, decent job. Don't mess that up for her."

"I just need a few minutes of her time."

Laura hesitated, then added, "Sarah wasn't just a witness, you know. She tried to tell the cops what she saw back then. Nobody listened."

That was interesting. "What did she see?"

"Not my story to tell. But if it's about that Reynolds guy who disappeared, she definitely saw something that night. Something that scared her enough that she quit working evenings for almost a year after."

I thanked Laura and headed for my car. The Blue Plate was about twenty minutes away, on the outskirts of town near the airport. If I hurried, I could catch Sarah before her shift ended.

THE BLUE PLATE was a classic American diner—chrome exterior, red vinyl booths, and a counter with swivel stools. A bell jingled as I entered, and the smell of coffee and fried food enveloped me. The lunch rush was winding down, with only a few tables still occupied.

A middle-aged waitress approached with a coffeepot. "Just one?"

"Actually, I'm looking for Sarah Jenkins. Is she working today?"

The waitress eyed me suspiciously. "Who's asking?"

I was getting tired of that question, but I understood the protective instinct. I showed her my license. "Harry Starke, private investigator. It's about a case she might have information on."

"Wait here." She disappeared through a swinging door to the kitchen.

A moment later, a woman in her early forties emerged, wiping her hands on her apron. Sarah Jenkins had blue eyes and a determined set to her jaw. Her brown hair was streaked with gray and pulled back in a practical ponytail.

"Mr. Starke?" She gestured to a booth in the far corner. "Peggy says you want to talk to me."

I nodded. She nodded back, and I followed her to the booth, noting that she chose the seat with its back to the wall, giving her a clear view of the entire diner.

"Thank you for seeing me," I began. "I'm investigating the disappearance of Michael Reynolds fifteen years ago."

She stiffened almost imperceptibly. "That case is back in the news. They found his body at the old factory."

"Yes," I replied. "And the men responsible were arrested last night trying to remove his remains."

Sarah poured coffee for both of us, though I hadn't asked for any. Her hands were steady, but I noticed the tightness around her eyes.

"Laura from The Sorbonne said you might have witnessed

something the night Reynolds disappeared, and that you tried to tell the police about it."

She took a deep breath. "I did. Nobody took me seriously. Just a waitress in a dive bar—what could I possibly know, right?"

"I'm taking you seriously," I assured her. "Tell me what you saw that night."

Sarah glanced around the diner, then leaned forward, lowering her voice. "It was a Wednesday night, slow for The Sorbonne. Reynolds was a semi-regular—came in maybe once a week, usually alone, had a couple of beers, left a good tip. Polite guy, not like most of the clientele."

"You seem to remember him well," I said.

"Hard to forget someone when their disappearance is all over the news." She sipped her coffee. "That night, he was there early, maybe seven o'clock. Seemed anxious, kept checking his watch. Then this other guy comes in, wearing an expensive suit —looked completely out of place. Reynolds waved him over."

"Victor Harmon?" I asked.

She nodded. "I didn't know his name then, but I recognized him when his picture was in the paper later. They sat in a booth near the back, but I could still hear bits of their conversation when I brought their drinks."

"What were they saying?"

"Reynolds was angry, saying something about numbers not adding up and government contracts. The suit—Harmon— kept telling him to calm down, that he was misunderstanding the situation." She frowned, concentrating on the memory. "Reynolds said something like, 'I have copies of everything. Either you fix this, or I'm going to the FBI on Monday.'"

"How did Harmon react?"

"He got real quiet, then said something like, 'Let's discuss this somewhere more private.' Reynolds refused, said he didn't trust Harmon anymore."

"Did it get physical?"

Sarah shook her head. "Not there. But Harmon made a phone call before leaving. I heard him say, 'He's not being reasonable. Plan B.' Then he told Reynolds they'd finish the conversation at the factory, where he could show him the 'correct documentation.'"

"And Reynolds agreed?" I asked.

"Reluctantly. He left maybe five minutes after Harmon. Paid his bill, left me a good tip, said goodnight. That was the last time anyone saw him alive, as far as I know."

I made notes as she spoke. "Did you see anyone else unusual in the bar that night? Anyone who might have been watching their conversation?"

Sarah thought for a moment. "There was a guy at the bar. Big guy, military type. He didn't order much, just sat at the end of the bar nursing a beer and keeping his back to the room, but I caught him watching their reflection in the mirror behind the bar."

"Could it have been Raymond Powell? Head of security at CMI?"

"Maybe. I never got a clear look at his face. But he left right after Reynolds did."

"And you told the police all this?" I asked.

Her expression hardened. "I tried. A detective came around asking questions a few days later. Morris, I think his name was. I told him everything, but he seemed distracted, kept looking at his watch. Said he'd follow up, but nobody ever came back."

"Did anyone else ever ask you about that night? Anyone approach you afterward?"

She hesitated, then nodded slowly. "About a week later, a man came to The Sorbonne looking for me. Said he was from CMI, wanted to talk about company policy regarding employees in the bar. I told Benny I was sick and left through the back door. The guy came back twice more, then stopped."

"Did you recognize him?"

"No. But he gave me a bad feeling. After that, I switched to day shifts only. Six months later, I left The Sorbonne altogether."

I studied her carefully. "Sarah, would you be willing to make an official statement to the police? What you've told me could be crucial evidence connecting Harmon directly to Reynolds the night he disappeared."

She glanced around the diner again, a nervous habit. "I have a family now. A good life. I don't want trouble."

"These men killed a young man who was trying to expose their crimes, then spent fifteen years building wealth and power while his mother waited for answers. She's dying now, with only weeks to live. Your testimony could help ensure she sees justice for her son before she goes."

Sarah was quiet for a long moment, turning her coffee cup in her hands. Finally, she nodded. "Alright. I'll talk to the police. But I want to do it officially, with a lawyer present. No off-the-record conversations that can be forgotten later."

"I'll arrange it," I promised. "Lieutenant Kate Gazzara is leading the investigation. She's thorough and honest."

"One more thing, Mr. Starke." Sarah's eyes met mine directly. "That night, when Reynolds and Harmon were arguing, Reynolds said something that stuck with me. He said, 'It's not just the money, it's the technology. People could die if this gets out.' What did he mean by that?"

"Michael had discovered that CMI executives were not only embezzling funds from government contracts, but also stealing classified drone technology and selling modified versions for private profit," I explained. "Technology that was meant for military use only."

Sarah's eyes widened. "So he really was going to the FBI."

"Yes. And that's why they killed him. Not just to protect

their embezzlement scheme, but to prevent a national security issue from becoming public."

"My God." She shook her head slowly. "All these years, I wondered if what I heard that night really mattered. If I could have done something to save him."

"You tried," I reminded her. "The system failed, not you. But now you have another chance to help bring justice."

She nodded, resolute. "Tell Lieutenant Gazzara I'll be available whenever she needs me."

As I left the diner, I called Kate to relay what I'd learned. Sarah Jenkins' testimony placed Harmon with Reynolds just hours before his disappearance, arguing about the very issues that had led to the murder. More importantly, it established premeditation. "Plan B" suggested Harmon had already considered alternatives if Reynolds couldn't be persuaded to keep quiet.

The case against Harmon was solidifying. Lucan's involvement was clear from his attempted flight and the financial evidence. Powell had been caught at the scene. The only loose end was Martin Greene, still missing and potentially on the run.

As I drove back toward downtown, my phone rang. It was Tim.

"Harry, I found something on Greene. His credit card was just used to purchase a bus ticket from Atlanta to Miami. He must have driven to Atlanta last night to avoid being tracked leaving Chattanooga."

"Miami means he's probably heading for the Caribbean or South America," I reasoned. "When does the bus arrive?"

"Tonight, 8:45 PM."

"Contact Kate. Have her coordinate with Miami PD to have someone waiting at the bus station." I checked the time. "And see if you can track his phone. He might have ditched his regular cell, but most people carry a backup."

"Already on it," Tim assured me. "Also, you should know that Thomas Reynolds arrived in town an hour ago. He's at the hospice with his mother now."

"I'll head over there next. I want to brief him on what we've found."

The case was coming together rapidly now. With Sarah Jenkins' testimony establishing the connection between Harmon and Reynolds on the night of the murder, and the physical evidence from the factory, the prosecution had a strong case. If we could locate Martin Greene before he fled the country, we might get a complete confession that would ensure swift justice.

Eleanor Reynolds didn't have much time left. But it seemed increasingly likely that she would live to see her son's killers brought to account for their crimes.

EPILOGUE

Justice Served

ONE MONTH LATER, I STOOD BESIDE ELEANOR REYNOLDS' hospital bed. Despite the doctors' predictions, she had held on, determined to see justice for her son. Now, thin and frail but with clear eyes, she listened as I delivered the news she'd been waiting fifteen years to hear.

"The district attorney accepted plea deals from all four conspirators," I told her. "In exchange for avoiding the death penalty, they've provided full confessions."

A weak smile touched Eleanor's lips. "Tell me."

"It happened almost exactly as we pieced together. Michael discovered the financial fraud and technology theft at CMI. When he confronted Harmon, Lucan, Greene, and Lawson with evidence, they lured him to the factory that night. Lucan struck him with a pipe during the argument, killing him instantly."

"And Powell?" she asked.

"He handled the disposal of the body. They decided to bury Michael under the concrete floor that was being rein-forced the next day as part of planned renovations. Powell supervised the work himself, ensuring no questions were asked."

Eleanor closed her eyes briefly. "My poor boy."

"The technology theft was even worse than we suspected," I continued. "They were selling modified versions of classified military drone systems to private security firms and certain foreign entities. The FBI has opened a separate investigation."

"What sentences will they serve?" she asked.

"Harmon and Lucan got thirty years each for second-degree murder and conspiracy. Powell accepted twenty years in exchange for his full testimony. Greene got twenty-five years. Diane Lawson received fifteen years for her role in the conspiracy and coverup."

Eleanor nodded slowly. "It's done, then."

"Yes," I said, taking her thin hand in mine. "It's done. Michael can rest in peace now."

"And so can I." Her voice was barely audible.

Thomas Reynolds, who had been standing silently by the window, moved to his mother's side. "The funeral is arranged, Mom. Just as you wanted. Next to Dad."

"And Michael?"

"His remains will be released next week. We'll lay him to rest properly."

She smiled weakly. "Thank you, Mr. Starke. You kept your promise."

Three days later, Eleanor Reynolds passed away peacefully in her sleep. I attended her funeral, watching from a distance as she was laid to rest beside her husband. Her son's burial would follow once the authorities released his remains.

Back at my office, I closed the Reynolds file. The case that had gone cold for fifteen years had been solved in less than two weeks, bringing justice a month later for Michael and peace for his mother before she died.

"Tough case," Jacque commented, bringing me coffee.

"Aren't they all?" I replied. "In their own way?"

She lingered at my desk. "The DA sent something for you." She handed me an envelope.

Inside was a handwritten note from Eleanor Reynolds, dated the day after our final conversation:

Mr. Starke,

When I came to your office six weeks ago, I had lost all hope of ever knowing what happened to my Michael. Because of you, I can leave this world knowing the truth and seeing justice done. Some secrets stay buried forever, but not this one. Thank you for uncovering it.

With deepest gratitude, Eleanor Reynolds

I placed the note carefully in the case file before closing it for the last time. Outside my window, the sun was setting over Chattanooga, casting long shadows across the city. Somewhere in those shadows, other secrets were waiting to be uncovered, other wrongs waiting to be righted.

But for now, this case was complete, and justice had been served.

And in my business, that's the best you can hope for.

THANK you for reading this short story. I hope you enjoyed this novella with Harry Starke.

IF YOU WOULD LIKE to read more books with Harry Starke, I suggest Book One of Harry Starke The Early Years: Genesis Series, or Book One of the Harry Starke Novels Series. Keep reading for a full list of my books!

Book 1 of 9: Harry Starke Genesis

Book 1 of 24: The Harry Starke Novels

From Blair Howard

The Harry Starke Genesis Series
9 Books in Series as of 2025

The Harry Starke Series
24 Books in Series as of 2025

The Lt. Kate Gazzara Murder Files
21 Books in Series as of 2025

Randall And Carver Mysteries
3 Books in Series as of 2025

The Peacemaker Series
3 Books in Series as of 2025

The O'Sullivan Chronicles: Civil War Series
5 Books in Series as of 2025

From Blair C. Howard

The Sovereign Star Series
7 Books in Series as of 2025

1st three books are also available in German

ABOUT THE AUTHOR

Blair Howard is a retired journalist turned novelist. He's the author of more than 50 novels including the international best-selling Harry Starke series of detective crime stories, the Lt. Kate Gazzara Police Procedural series, the Harry Starke Genesis series, and the Randall & Carver Mysteries. He's also the author of the Peacemaker series of international spy thrillers and five Civil War/Western novels.

If you enjoy reading Science Fiction thrillers, Mr. Howard has made his debut into the genre with, The Sovereign Stars Series under the name, Blair C. Howard.

www.BlairHowardBooks.com